Have Yourself a Merry Little Collins

Katelyn Snyder

Content Warnings

This story contains content that might be troubling to some readers, including domestic violence (flashbacks and mentions of experiences from female main characters POV- on page), drunk driving (not of a main character), car accident (involving main characters-no injuries), death of a sibling (due to drunk driving-flashbacks from main characters POV), and graphic sexual content

Playlist

Potential-Lauv
    Ways to Go-Alec Benjamin (ft. Khalid)
    Make You Mine-PUBLIC
    Call Me When You Break Up- Selena Gomez, Benny
Blanco (with Gracie Abrams)
    the me I was-Kenzie
    I Wanna Love You (But I Don't)-Ashe
    dopamine-Zach Hood
    Mr. Brightside-The Killers
    sweat-Haiden Henderson
    Love Me For The Both Of Us-CJ Fam
    Good Luck, Babe!-Chappel Roan
    this is what slow dancing feels like-JVKE
    We Broke Up-Kelsea Ballerini
    Somebody's Heartbreak-Hunter Hayes
    Tennessee Whiskey-Austin Giorgio
    forever and a day-Abe Parker
    downbad duet-pj frantz and Elyse Myers

To The Men Who Love Women After Heartbreak-
Kelsea Ballerini

Prologue

Slamming doors. Name-calling. Refusing to speak to me. Isolation. Despite knowing that I deserve better, I willingly put myself through all these things. My friends are right, he's a horrible man, he doesn't love me, he just wants someone to control.

Today was the final straw.

I'm getting ready for Darcy's baby shower and Benji stands behind me as I freshen my curls and throw on my mascara. I turn to exit the room only for him to physically block my exit. My pulse immediately quickens, while my throat clogs.

"Where are you going?" He asks, leaning causally against the door frame—as if I haven't reminded him every day for the past week that I will be gone for a few hours today.

"Darcy's baby shower, I'll be back this afternoon and I'll text you, babe." I try to remain calm, inching my way towards the door, hopeful he will move out of my way. He doesn't.

"Just females right?"

"Yep, the guys have Huggies and Chuggies with the team." I have to physically keep my shoulders from bunching while I answer the question; if he senses my anxiety, he'll feed on it. Benji will sulk or make me feel like I'm abandoning him for spending time with the people I consider my family.

"Good, you know I don't want you around *him* anymore." His jaw ticks, refusing to say Collins' name. When he found out that Collins and I had been hanging out in my free time, Benji blew a gasket, throwing around words like cheater and whore, 'forbidding' me to be in his presence unless we were in a group setting, which I've stuck to... For the most part.

"I know, Benji, and I haven't been around him unless I had to be." I gently place my hand on his chest, lifting to place a kiss on his lips before attempting to move out of the bathroom and into the hallway of his apartment. I don't make it far before his large hand is wrapped around my wrist, and I'm pinned against the hallway wall by his broad body. The slight moment of peace I thought I was experiencing shatters immediately.

"Listen to me, and you better listen fucking well." His voice is dark and low in my ear. "If you come back here looking like you've been touched, smelling like another man, or a minute later than you say you will be... Well, I think you know how angry that will make me." Benji's grip loosens, one hand moves to my hip, and the other gently strokes my cheek. "And you don't want me to be angry, do you, Baby?"

"No, I never want to make you angry." I try to smile, but I'm sure it's more of a grimace.

"Well, you do make me angry, most days, I need you to stop doing that. I can't be with someone who doesn't consider my feelings." I fight not to throw his words back at him, as he's never considered my feelings once over the past year. The gentle hand on my cheek moves to my chin and becomes a firm grasp, holding me in place.

"You're hurting me." I manage the anxiety coming back full force as I look into the dark eyes of the man who has had control over my life for the past year.

"Do you think I care? Like I said, you make me angry every day, and, Harley, right now I'm pissed because I know that you're lying." His grip tightens a little more as he glares down at me. Benji has never hit me, but he will hold me tightly in place while he seethes and screams in my face. Something that I've unfortunately become accustomed to.

"Benji, babe, I promise that I wouldn't do that to you." I try to push on his chest, but he's too strong for me, keeping me firmly where he wants me.

"Oh, but H, I know better, and that's why I've decided you're going to stay here with me." He backs away from me, giving me a little space in this tiny apartment hallway.

"No." I rebuke, surprising even myself with how firm my tone is. I've never once told him no, but I'm tired and want to celebrate my friend. "I'm going to the baby shower and I will come back afterward."

"What?" He snarls but doesn't close in on me again. I

take this opportunity to scurry down the hallway toward the apartment door. "You're. Not. Leaving."

"I am going. If you try to stop me, I will not come back." As I'm unlocking the front door, Benji's large hand presses against it, holding it shut.

"Baby, come on. I asked you not to go." His voice is suddenly smooth and sweet again, attempting to manipulate me into staying with him.

"No, you demanded that I stay." I sigh, but don't turn to face him. However, I do notice that his palm is no longer flat against the door. It's clenched into a fist, and his breathing is getting heavier. "I'm going now, I will text you when I get there and let you know when I'll be back."

His fist thwacks against the door, causing me to jump before it drops back to his side, "Harley. Please don't leave, I just want to hang out with you."

I take the opportunity to swing the door open, but before I can make it through the door frame, his arms are banding around my waist in what a passerby might assume was a hug if they didn't know he was trying to keep me in his apartment.

"Benji, let go, please." I attempt to soothe his temper by running my hands up his arms, it's worked before, but this time, it doesn't. I don't struggle because it won't do anything to keep him semi-tolerable.

"I'm just going to miss you." I can hear the tension in his voice, the way he's holding onto his last string of control before he begins fully throwing a tantrum.

"I'll miss you too, babe. The sooner I go, though, the sooner I can be back in your arms." He doesn't respond, instead taking a step back and kicking the door closed before setting me on my feet and spinning me to face him.

"Promise me that you're coming back to me?" He begs, and I know he means it. He's scared I'm going to leave and never return, despite knowing that every other time I've threatened not to come back, I end up right back here. With him.

"Promise." I smile softly at him, then I'm pushed back against the wall, and his hands are all over me, his lips on my neck. With anyone else, I would love that, but his tongue feels scratchy against my skin. "Benji, I've got to go."

Rather than letting up, he presses his pelvis into mine and continues to run his hands along my body, "Don't leave me."

"I'll be back," I sigh.

"I need you, do you feel what you do to me?" He ruts himself against me again, and I attempt to push him away. He looks up at me first with shock that quickly morphs into rage. Before holding his body firmer against mine, my leg between his presents the perfect opportunity. I swiftly lift my knee into his crotch, and he doubles over in pain, so I do it again, but to his nose. He falls to the ground.

"You fucking bitch." He groans as I grab my purse, slam the door, and run down the hallway and then the stairs to my car. Panicked breaths heave in and out of my mouth. Tears stream down my face, but I don't slow down until I'm pulled out of his apartment complex and speeding in the direction of the one person that I know can calm me down in this situation.

The door to Collins' modest suburban home swings open. His brows raise in confusion and then dip in concern when he sees my state. I'm sure my makeup is running down my face, and my clothes are probably wrinkled. "Harley, are you okay?"

"No." I gulp in a breath, the adrenaline beginning to wear off.

"What's wrong?"

"I left." I don't have to tell him who I left, why I left, or what happened. Collins is the only person in my life who truly knows what I have been dealing with when it comes to Benji. Collins lifts me into his arms. Just like every other time I've shown up here in tears, he carries me to the couch, pulling me into his side, where I cry, then I speak. Recounting the entire situation to him through my tears, I notice as his free hand clenches into a fist and then unclenches repeatedly at his side. He's never liked Benji, yet he's always been supportive when I need it.

"Aren't you supposed to be at the baby shower?" He asks rather than forcing me to talk more about what happened.

"Well, yes, but I can't go in this condition. I'm unwell and Darcy probably already hates me." A new ache in my chest forms where the adrenaline once was. My friends have done their best to support me, despite how I've abandoned them.

"I promise they're just worried about you. I think they'd love to see you." His voice is like a warm cup of chamomile tea; it calms me in ways I don't understand.

"I'm late. Kodi tried to call me while I was on my way here, but I could barely breathe, let alone have a conversation with my best friends." I argue. I know they'd love to see me, but then I'd have to rehash it again. I don't think I'm ready for that.

"She'll understand. I can follow you to the beach house if you want." His strong hand that's wrapped around my side runs softly up and down my arm.

"No, you have to get to Tate's party," I say, burrowing further into his side before we stand. He grabs the box of Huggies from beside the door, and we walk to our cars.

Collins always opens my car door for me, but before I slide in, he says, "Text me when you get there, and come back here if you don't want to go home tonight. Either way, just let me know, okay?"

"Of course. Thank you, Collins," I say, wrapping my arms around him before sliding into my car and heading toward Tatum's beach bungalow. Watching the ocean crash against the bridge and the sunset along the horizon reminds me of something I often share with my clients at the Right Place, Right Time Center. A quote by Ralph Waldo Emerson, "Every sunset brings the promise of a new dawn."

Chapter 1

Earth to Harls

Harley ǁ Present day

Since leaving Benji eleven months ago, he's been texting and calling relentlessly, but I refuse to respond; luckily, he hasn't shown up at my place or my job. Eleven months of actually being able to show up for my friends. Being able to heal and enjoy my life, post Benji or P.B., as we've been calling it. Being able to watch Bella, Kodi and Mav's daughter, and Hayden, Darcy and Tate's son grow up. I'm actually able to commit to traveling to the Smoky Mountains with my best friends for Christmas this year.

"Earth to Harls." Kodi snaps her fingers at me across the fire pit on her back porch. It's Tuesday, so I'm at Kodi and Mav's for a family dinner—although they're not family by blood, my friends are my family by choice. The guys from the team and my besties, including the newest member of the team Conrad Hoyer, his girlfriend Enid, and her younger brother, Mace are all here to prep for our upcoming trip.

"Huh? Yep. What's up?" I stutter, hoping I wasn't missing an important conversation.

"Your time off got approved, right?" Darcy asks from where she stands, bouncing Hayden to sleep.

"Yes! I'm so excited to spend Christmas with you all," I beam at them.

Sin claps excitedly, "Yay! That means everyone's going to come!"

"There's an innuendo in there somewhere..." Darcy smirks, proud of herself.

"If you weren't holding my nephew, I would throw a pillow at your head," I laugh, and her grin widens.

"Speaking of coming, Harley and Sin, are you bringing anyone with you? We have to figure out sleeping arrangements. There's a main cabin, a two-bedroom, and then a small A-frame big enough for two people," Kodi prods.

"Absolutely not, I'm happy to spend the week with just you guys. No extra penises or vaginas necessary." Sin sounds appalled, her face screwing up in disgust like the idea of having a partner at Christmas time is the worst thing in the world.

"Nope, just me this year." I smile, but Kodi's eyebrows furrow. I wouldn't mind having someone to cuddle up next to the fire and watch all the classics with though. My brain betrays me when a certain, red-headed, left-winger runs by with Bella on his back. Her loud laugh fills the space, and his smile broadens.

"Are you sure you're okay? If Benji is still around, we can-"

Immediately, I feel the need to squash my friend's thinking that I'd give him another chance. I refuse to do that.

"I need to fess up to something." I cut Ko off and feel four sets of eyes burning into my soul. Before I can even think about something rational—like just telling them that Benji is long gone—I'm concocting a tale about someone that I know they'll approve of. "Collins... Collins and I can take the A-frame together—because we've been seeing each other for a little bit."

Grace, Mav's sister, covers her shocked expression with her glass of wine. Kodi's eyes are the size of saucers while Darcy and Sinclair don't look impressed or convinced.

"How long?" Darcy questions.

"A month or two," I throw out, cataloging these details so that when I go to Collins and beg him to help me convince our friends we're in a relationship, I can make sure he knows how this developed.

"And you've been hiding it this whole time?" Grace is the next to speak.

"We've been keeping it private, the whole Benji thing kind of threw a wrench into how I handle my relationships going forward."

"I don't buy it," Sin, my best friend and the one who'd be able to call me on my bullshit, asserts. Her arms are crossed over her chest, and she's shooting laser beams into my irises. "I'm going to call him over, surely he'll want to fess up, considering we'll find out in the mountains anyway."

"No—" I fish for a good reason, "just let me talk to him

before you out us to the whole group. You know how shy he is."

"How did this happen?" Now it's Kodi's turn to see if I falter.

"As you know, he's always been a support system for me, a safe place to go when things would get too difficult."

"We could've been that for you, too, you know?" Sin sounds hurt, and I can't blame her. Rather than going to my best friend when I was struggling, I ran to someone we met less than two years ago.

"I know, I'm sorry."

"So after Benji, you were still hanging out?" Sin continues to prod for holes in my story.

"Yes, I was at his house all the time, not just to check on Precious while they were away for games. So much so that he was keeping my favorite snacks, tampons, and coffee creamer stocked." *Wait a minute... Nope. Not thinking about how thoughtful that is.* "It just kind of naturally progressed. The more time we spent together and the more comfortable I got, the easier it was to see that there was potential for more. So we're exploring that."

"Why fess up now, then? Rather than just sneaking around in the mountains." Darcy narrows her eyes at me, and I begin to sweat a little bit as she scrutinizes me.

"I've kept too much from you guys over the past year, and what better way to spend Christmas than cuddled up into a cute hockey player's side?" I mean both of those statements wholeheartedly.

"Fine, but I won't believe it until I see it." Enid, who's normally the passive one, says. Her eyes flitting back and forth between me and Collins. She briefly pauses, smiling softly at Conrad and Mace tossing a football back and forth. *Ironic.*

"Ladies, may I top you off?" Dominic bows as he opens the sliding glass door, holding a freshly opened bottle of white. Rather than responding, we all hold our glasses out for him as he pours. He lingers in front of Sin a moment longer than the rest of us before setting the bottle on the side table and joining the guys back in the grass.

"Okay, so roomie assignments. The Harts, the Reeds, the parents, the future Hoyers, plus Nik and Dom will take the big cabin. Grace and Jason can take the two-bedroom cabin with Sin. Then Collins and Harls get the A-frame. Does that work for everyone?" Kodi asks, seeking confirmation that everyone is comfortable with the arrangements. Of course, I'm comfortable with that; Collins and I have slept in the same vicinity before. Nothing crazy is going to happen if we sleep in the same bed for a week and a half.

"That works for me. Wait. Grace," Sin lowers her voice, "are you guys loud?"

"Oh my God! Sin! You can't just ask people that." I screech.

"What! I'm just making sure I don't need to bring my noise-canceling headphones for nighttime. The holidays make men ravenous." Sin's mischievous laugh bursts from her mouth.

"You may want to bring them," Grace says straight-faced. In the next moment, we're all doubled over, gasping for air from laughing so hard. All of the men have now turned their heads in our direction, causing us to straighten up, doing our best to act casual.

"Grace, you dirty dog. I knew you would fit in with us." Sin hums.

"I am so ready for this trip and some uninterrupted time with everyone." Kodi sighs contentedly.

"Cheers," I say as I hold my wine glass into the air, waiting for everyone to clink theirs with mine.

"Where are you headed?" Sin asks me as she pours coffee into the biggest mug I've ever seen. She's preparing to work her first twelve hours of the week, and the coffee will be needed.

"Collins' place." I smile at her.

"Harls," she probes.

"Sin," I purr back.

She pours an obscene amount of peppermint mocha creamer into her coffee as she speaks, "I don't buy it."

"Jesus, Sin. Can you even taste the coffee anymore?"

"That's the whole point, I like my creamer with a side of coffee." She shrugs, "Stop avoiding my statement."

"Just because something is private doesn't make it untrue, Sin. I have to go, Precious is expecting me." I smile devilishly at my best friend, blowing her a kiss and turning toward the front door.

"We'll see about that!" Sinclair shouts at my back.

The entire drive to Collins' house, I replay last night and the talk with the girls, all the details to make sure I can relay them properly to *my boyfriend*. He won't say no, right?

Chapter 2

Oh, Look, Mac N' Cheese

Collins

Precious begins scratching at the front door as soon as the doorbell rings; she knows that Harley has arrived. I just finished plating our elevated mac n' cheese, meaning I seasoned boxed mac and added protein to it, along with a veggie on the side.

Upon opening the door, Harley stands there, her dark brown curls pulled out of her face, some hanging loosely. Every time her eyes meet mine, my breath is stolen from my lungs. Something about Harley Wheeler keeps me enraptured, even doing the most mundane things.

"Hey, Peppermint." I greet, trying not to smile too widely in her presence. She quirks a brow at my nickname but has yet to ask me where it came from.

"Hi, Collins. Precious!" She scoops my cat into her arms, walking further into my small home. Precious immediately nuzzles into her chest.

"Just finished dinner."

"Oh, yay! I'm starving. Sinclair was scrutinizing me before I left, so I didn't eat." She shrugs it off as if I'm not going to prod for more information.

"Scrutinized you because..." Leaving it open-ended, hoping that, as she usually does, she'll spill the reasoning.

"Um, no reason in particular."

"Harls, why are you being so weird?"

"Me? Weird? Never! Oh, look, mac n' cheese." Harley swipes the bowls of macaroni, while I grab two sparkling water bottles from my fridge and leading me to the couch, where I sit befuddled.

Harley and I can house food together, but the way she devours this mac n' cheese to avoid talking to me has me replaying the last few days. *Did I miss something?*

"Do you have a fever?" I set my bowl down and reach for her forehead.

"No."

"Well, you need to talk to me because whatever is happening here," I gesture to the area where she sits with my hand, "is freaking me out."

"I don't even know how to start this conversation." She bemoans, and my brain automatically spirals into worries for her safety.

"Did something happen with—"

"No!"

"Okay, good."

"Alright, so you know that big trip we're all taking together in a few weeks?" She asks sheepishly.

"Yep, I'm pretty sure my bank account does too." We both chuckle lightly when I say this.

It's then that the floodgates open and I'm assaulted with

an onslaught of Harley's panic-ridden words, "When the girls and I were talking last night about the trip, and just life in general. They've just been asking me over and over if I'm okay. Then, when I told them I wasn't bringing anyone to the trip, they assumed it was because I went back to Benji! Which hell fucking no, would I even consider doing that *ever* again. Then they asked me again if I was okay, and like, hello, yes, I'm perfectly fine. I mean, I guess not perfectly fine, but okay enough, and like I'm here. I've been here for months! Anyway, I maybe, possibly, told them that you and I needed a cabin together because we've been seeing each other for a few months. That's why Sinclair was giving me the third degree before I came over today; she doesn't believe me. At all."

For a moment, my world stops spinning. The girl that I've been in love with for months just said she told her friends we were dating, because, well, I don't know why. I think I forgot everything else that she had said before saying she told them we were dating.

"Oh my God, Collins, I am so sorry. I can't believe I did that. You know what? I'm going to text them and tell them right now that I was lying because I'm tired of them checking on me and only me." Harley's frantic tone pulls me back to reality just in time to grab her wrist and stop her from texting them.

"No, wait. It's okay." I try to keep my tone even as I speak, "It's just for two weeks, right? We can manage that."

"It's not just two weeks, Collins. It's the entire time leading up to the trip, during the trip, and maybe even after. We can't just break up after the trip."

"I'll do it."

"You'll pretend to be my boyfriend?" Her eyebrows are in her hairline, like it's so hard for her to comprehend that I would want to spend more of my free time with her than I already do.

"Yes." I throw out with no hesitation before adding, "The guys have been bothering me about dating, too, so it'll take some heat off both our backs."

"Okay, now what?"

"I think we need to start going on some 'dates'," I suggest, selfishly begging for more alone time with her.

"Collins, I think we'll be fine."

"No, if you want to sell this. Some things are going to have to change, Harls." I emphasize.

"What do you mean?"

"I mean," I scoot closer to her. Our thighs barely touching sends my pulse skyrocketing, "You need to get used to me being this close so that my touches don't send you scooting away from me." Hesitantly, I wrap my arm around her shoulder, pulling her into my side, fingers caressing up and down her arm. She fits perfectly here; she *belongs* in this empty space.

Harley sucks in a breath as I continue, "I mean that while we've been hanging out alone for a while and we platonically cuddle, we have to make it look more romantic around our friends. That I need to plan dates, bring you flowers, touch you more casually, and vice versa."

"That's probably a good idea." She concedes.

"Friday night? I'll pick you up and we can go to the drive-in." I don't know if she remembers telling me this, but she's always wanted to go on a date to a drive-in movie—as we know, Benji was never going to take her there. Now's my time to shine.

"What movies are playing?" She asks and I pull up my phone to search what's playing. I already know what's playing, and I already know it's one of her favorites because I was going to ask her if she wanted to go before this whole scheme came about.

"Some rom-com from the nineties that's a play off of Taming of the Shrew. Sounds right up your alley. Or Scream, but I know horror isn't your fave."

"Ten Things I Hate About You!" She squeaks in delight, "I love that movie. Yes, we'll watch that one."

"Anything you want, Peppermint."

Chapter 3

Easy as Breathing

Harley

Thank fuck he agreed. I mean, I figured he would, but this is fake, it's to prove to my friends that I'm okay. That's it.

I say that as I prepare for my first official 'date' with my boyfriend. Struggling to decide what I want to wear to the drive-in movie theatre. I need to be comfortable but cute.

"Sinclair!" I half groan, half scream across the hallway where her bedroom door sits open.

"What!" She hollers back. This is a normal occurrence in our apartment.

"Help."

Five seconds later, Sinclair has stepped into my bedroom.

"I don't know what to wear on my date."

"How about nothing?" She wiggles her eyebrows at me.

"Maybe after my date, but considering I don't want a public nudity charge, clothes would be preferred."

"Where's he taking you?"

"Drive-in! My fave nineties movie is playing."

"Oh, fun! I'd say something cute and comfy then. Maybe leggings, sneakers, and a cute sweater? That way, you can sit comfortably in the back of the Tacoma."

"You're a genius." I grab her head, kissing the top before stepping into my closet and grabbing some sweater options.

"Green." She says after a moment of looking between the three I pulled out.

"Oh! I forgot I grabbed you something to pack for our trip the other day." Sin's mischievous grin can't mean anything good for me. "Be right back."

While she's gone, I finish getting changed and begin pulling half of my hair back, leaving some curls sitting around my face.

"Here ya go." She throws a black box onto the bed beside me where I'm tying my shoes.

"Sin, what is this?" I can tell just by looking at the box, but I don't understand why my best friend is gifting me a sex toy.

"Something for the cabin. I'm sure you and Collins could have a lot of fun with this. Since you'll have a lot of alone time with your new beau, obviously sex is going to ensue."

My cheeks heat instantly. It's clear that everyone is going to be expecting us to bang it out in the cabin. However, my mind betrays me by putting an image of a very sweaty, very muscular, and very hard Collins into my head, making me think this toy may get some use before our trip.

"Sin." I sigh, shaking the dirty image from my head and

sliding the box onto my bedside table without a second glance.

"Harls."

"Why?"

"As I said before, lots of time to play with each other, figured this could bring a little spice in." She shrugs as if gifting sex toys is normal.

Before I can respond, three heavy knocks resound throughout the apartment. Collins is here to rescue me from my best friend's shenanigans. Thank God.

I swing the door open and am hit by Collins' cologne, leather, and masculine. I'm also greeted by the most beautiful bouquet of purple tulips.

"Harley." He smiles at me, surveying my outfit briefly. Pulling me into his arms and placing a kiss on my forehead.

"Collins." I can't help but smile as I pull back.

"You look beautiful, these are for you." He hands me the flowers quickly, perusing my body once more. Heat flares in his eyes, but he quickly blinks it away.

"Thank you, let me get them in water. Then we can go."

"I can take care of those. You two go have fun." Sin says from behind me, eyeing us both closely.

"Oh... Okay, thanks." I hand them to her before grabbing my purse and letting Collins take my hand, guiding me down to his truck.

"Are you sure we can get away with this?" I ask as Collins pulls into a spot in the theatre, his bed facing the giant, white screen.

"Definitely can." He reassures me, placing a hand on my thigh, which causes my blood to boil immediately.

I lean over and place a quick kiss on his cheek, "Easy as breathing. We do this all the time."

"Easy as breathing." He smirks before hopping out of the truck, "Stay here. It's a little chilly, let me get everything set up, then you can join me in the back."

A few moments later my door is opened, and Collins is helping me out of the truck. He leads me around the back, where pillows and blankets line the plastic bed. An assortment of popcorn, sour and sweet snacks, and waters sit in what I like to call a snackle box.

"Collins, this is perfect."

"You deserve nothing but the best, Harls." His voice is closer than I expected, and then his arms are wrapped around me from behind as I take in the area he's set up for us. "Let's get you in there."

His hands move to my waist, easily lifting me into the bed of the truck, and I scoot toward the back, as he follows behind me.

"What else do you think is missing to pull this off?" I ask, pulling a sour candy from the box and sticking it into my mouth. My mouth twists up from the punch of the sour treat almost immediately.

He doesn't speak for a moment, then says, "Sure, we have platonic cuddles and have slept in the same bed, but we've never kissed Harls. You know our friends won't buy it if we aren't affectionate with each other. They haven't seen either of us with partners in a while."

I wonder if the same thoughts I'm having cross his mind. Hoping that he suggests we kiss partially because it's true and partially because he's as desperate to feel my lips on his as I am his.

"Let's kiss then, get the first one out of the way," I say boldly.

A groan sounds deep in Collins' throat before his body turns toward mine.

"Fuck it." He mutters before his hands bracket my face, and he leans toward me. Without hesitation, I find myself leaning into him as well. Our lips meet, Collins' thumb gently caressing my cheek as our lips move softly together for a moment. I find myself relaxing into his touch, sighing into his mouth, and wanting to push this kiss further. I don't get the opportunity because he pulls away, eyes glossed over and breathing just as heavy as mine.

"I don't think doing that regularly will be a problem." I try to laugh it off, but the way my body still feels like it's been lit on fire from that brief interaction makes my laugh waver.

"Agreed." He breathes, clearing his throat before shifting his body back toward the screen and pulling me into his side.

We spend the rest of the movie cuddled up like this, his strong arm wrapped around my shoulder and my head resting on his. The sounds of Patrick and Kat's banter and the low hum of vehicle engines filling the night air.

"Did you have fun tonight?" Collins asks as we pull up in front of my apartment building.

"Of course." I squeeze his hand, which he wrapped around mine as soon as he finished clearing the bed of the truck and started the drive back.

"Me too. Let's plan for once a week until the trip?" The question hangs in the air for a moment, which means three more dates. Erm... Fake dates. Probably the best ones I've ever been on, considering how perfect tonight was.

"That sounds great. Surely, they'll have to believe it by then, right?"

"I think so," Collins reassures. "I'll walk you up."

"You don't have to."

"I know I don't have to, but I want to." He adds, "Plus, you know Sin will kill me if she knows I let you walk up in the dark."

"I guess that's true."

When I go to grab my door handle, Collins, exiting the driver's side, says, "Don't you dare open that door. We have to break that habit; you should never have been doing that yourself."

I stop my movements immediately, the assertiveness in Collin's voice doing something to my body that it definitely shouldn't be. I don't have time to ponder it because the passenger door swings open and a hand is extended to assist me out.

The walk up to my apartment is quick, but our goodbye lingers as if the line we crossed earlier tonight is holding us in place. Collins pulls me into him, placing a quick kiss on my lips.

"She's watching." He says quietly against my lips.

"Probably. Thank you for tonight." I whisper back, our lips touching again as I speak.

"Goodnight, Peppermint." He says, pulling away and waiting for me to go in and lock the door behind me.

"Goodnight, Freckles."

Chapter 4

Maybe Steal a Kiss or Two

Collins

"Heard you and Harley have taken things public." Mav slaps a hand down on my shoulder as he passes by my locker, referring to the two dates we've gone on since entering our faux relationship.

"Where'd ya hear that?" I prod, knowing it was most definitely Kodi, his wife.

"Yeah, dude, why didn't you tell us about you and Harley?" Conrad speaks up from beside me.

"We've been taking things slow. The whole situation with her ex kind of threw things off a little bit. We've been going at her pace." I say, opting not to out her situation to the guys, it's not their business unless she wants it to be.

"That's fair, but why now?" Nik booms from across the locker room.

"I want to be able to love on my girl on our trip, especially at Christmas time. Sneaking around with everyone present was kind of going to be impossible." I shrug it off, surely that's a good enough excuse.

"Hmm... That makes sense." Dom hums decidedly.

"Everyone's still coming over for dinner tomorrow, right?" Mav asks, changing the subject.

A chorus of yeses resounds from around us.

"You're hiding something," Conrad says quietly as he's tying his skates.

I don't get to respond because Coach is hollering at us to get onto the ice for the morning skate.

Fuck. We're going to have to be convincing tomorrow.

I attempted to convince Harley and Sin to let me pick them up for dinner, but Sin insisted she drive herself. She argued that it was a Friday night, so surely Harley would be coming to spend the weekend with me. I hadn't even thought about that, but after a quick text exchange with Harls, she's bringing her weekend bag, and we'll have a lazy weekend. No pressure, no fancy clothes. Just us, Precious, and junk food.

I'm one of the first to arrive at Maverick's, pulling up behind Nik's motorcycle. I grab the s'mores dip from the passenger seat. I was charged with bringing it since it's too warm for a fire this evening.

As I walk up to the front door of Kodi and Maverick's suburban home, I pull my phone out to text Harley.

Deciding that Sin is more than likely going to be reading over her shoulder, I lay it on thick.

COLLINS

Hey, Baby, you going to be here soon? I miss you.

I'm guessing that the use of baby has sent a very cute and very pink blush across her skin. I wish I could see it.

HARLEY

Be there in 5.

There's a pause.

HARLEY

Miss you, too.

COLLINS

See you soon.

We don't even knock to enter the Hart residence anymore, just open the door using the assigned key code and head inside. I kick my shoes off next to the others before heading down the hall toward the living area. A few things have changed in the home since Kodi and Maverick married. She's updated the photos that line the entryway to include more of the friend group and her Mom. There are also more pops of color throughout the entire home, giving it a brighter feel.

I plop the dip onto the kitchen counter just before Bella barrels across the living room and into my barely waiting arms.

"Uncle Collins!" Bella's shrill voice fills the space. The

kid is so fast that I was just able to bend down and scoop her up.

"Hi, sweet girl. I missed you." I smile down at my pseudo-niece, planning to soak up all of her attention until Dom gets here and inevitably complains that I'm hanging with her. Unfortunately for him, she's not so little anymore and has her Mama's attitude, so if she doesn't want to sit next to you during dinner or play dinosaurs with you, she'll tell you right to your face. It kind of stings.

"You did?" She beams back at me.

"Of course, I did. I haven't seen you in... Seven sleeps. That's *so* many."

"You know what's so many sleeps?"

"How many?" I ask.

"Thirty."

"That's how old your Uncle Tatum is," I say a little louder than necessary as the front door opens. I know it's Tatum, Darcy, and Hayden based on the babbling noises echoing down the hallway.

"Ew, that's so old." Bella giggles more.

"Ouch, Bella. And Collins, my knees and back hurt, man, don't rub it in." Tatum laughs as he slaps my arm before taking Hayden into the living room and setting him on the carpet to play.

"Your girl is here. Go help her with her stuff." Darcy nudges me, taking Bella from my arms easily.

"Thanks." I turn on my heel, walk out the front door, and head out to the road where Sin's burnt orange Rav4 is parked.

"Collins," Sin smiles at me as she passes and heads inside.

Harley steps out of the car in ripped jeans and a tight black t-shirt. Her curls are messily pulled to the top of her head, and light makeup covers her face. I approach her where she's standing at the open passenger door.

"Hi, Baby." I can't keep myself from saying it, and just like I hoped, her cheeks pinken and she shies away from my look.

"I'm not going anywhere, you have to be able to look at me, Harls." I gently grab her chin, bringing her gaze back up to mine, "There she is."

"Hi." Her voice is timid as she stares back into my eyes, "Your shirt's nice."

"Thank you." I chuckle because I only have on a simple, green Henley, "Let's put your bag in my car and then head inside."

After stopping at my truck, I take Harley's hand and guide her into the house and to our place at the dining room table, where everyone waits for us.

"There's the lovebirds." Dom chides as we step into the house.

"We've been waiting on you two," Kodi adds, wiggling her eyebrows.

Harley's cheeks flush immediately, and I find myself protectively pulling her into my side.

"Just needed to check in on my girl. I missed her." I throw it out into the room.

"Check in. Sureeeee." Mace, the sarcastic teen brother of Enid, adds with a gesture mimicking quotations.

"Yes, just check in." I assert.

"Maybe steal a kiss or two." Sin adds, her tone questioning.

"None of your business. Let's eat." Harley puts the conversation to bed; she typically doesn't assert herself like this. I find myself beaming with pride.

"Okay... Tonight we've got ribs and whatever sides you heathens brought. Everything is set up like usual, get your food and be merry." Maverick booms, and we all break away to plate our food before reconvening in the dining space.

"Everyone ready for our trip?" Enid asks after we've all settled in and begun picking at our plates.

"Just about. I need to get little Mrs.Thing some warmer clothes before we head out." Kodi says about Bella.

"Do you wanna build a snowman?" Bella sings directly to Mace, who has become her new best friend since he introduced her to *all* of his turtle friends at Shell Shock'd— where he and Enid work.

"We can build a snowman, Bells." Mace insists.

"Nooo. You have to sing it back." Bella whines.

Mace blushes with embarrassment. He tries to act cool but we've all noticed that Bella and Hayden are his weak spots.

"Bella Bear, I don't think Mace wants to sing right now. It's so exciting that he wants to build a snowman with you, though!" Darcy pipes up, earning a mouthed thank you from Mace.

"Any ideas for food while we're up there?" Nik asks, he's the cook of the group, always willing to feed us. I think it's his secret love language.

"Dale volunteered to make chili, but that's pretty much all we have planned so far. We figured that Kodi, Bella, and I could hit a grocery store on the way up and then split the costs from there." Maverick responds.

"I think we need to do s'mores," Harley adds.

"That's not a meal, Baby." I chuckle.

"Anything can be a girl dinner." She volleys back.

"How about we do easy meals for a lot of people? Things like spaghetti, sliders, and tacos." Tatum suggests.

"I think those are all solid options and easy enough. I think I'll prep some pierogis beforehand." Nik asserts.

"Oh, yes." Dom moans, making everyone turn in his direction, confusion etched into all of their eyes.

"Don't make it weird, Dom." Conrad goads while laughs float throughout the room.

"I've been waiting years for this experience. Everyone else says they're delicious, and I've yet to experience them myself." Sin pipes up in excitement.

"They are!" All of the guys, including myself, say at once.

The rest of the evening goes by in a flurry. Everyone is so excited about our trip, we leave in just under three weeks. I know I shouldn't be as excited as I am about having Harley alone for a week, considering she isn't truly mine, but I'm ready for it.

Chapter 5

Fake or Not

Harley

My weekend with Collins goes by in a flash, we spent it just as promised–in our pajamas, cuddled up with Precious, and watching Lord of the Rings.

As Sunday rolled around, I found myself not wanting to leave his home. I feel comfortable, safe, and happy in his presence, like I don't need anyone or anything else when we're together.

Luckily, I only had to go five nights without him. It's not like we didn't talk or text, but being with him is different. He suggested we share one more date before leaving for the Smoky Mountains in a few weeks, so I'm getting myself ready for a dancing date with my boyfriend. I find myself letting my curls be free, slipping on a tight pair of ripped jeans, a black lace corset top, and sneakers. Heels are not made for dancing and that's what I plan to do tonight.

"Harls! Your man's here... And he looks scrumptious,

better get out here before I steal him for myself." Sin yells down the hallway.

"Don't you dare!" I find myself genuinely meaning the words, Collins is mine–fake or not.

"Feisty, I like it." She purrs back.

"I'll be there in a second!" I grab my wallet and phone before rushing down the hallway.

Holy shit. Sin was not lying. Collins stands in our entryway wearing black slacks that hug his thighs and a deep grey button-up that's rolled up his forearms. The veins protruding from those forearms are porn worthy and I want to run my tongue along them... Along with somewhere else on his body.

"You look..." I start to say, but my mouth is too dry to get anything else out.

"You too, Peppermint." Collins winks, "Ready?"

"To beat off all the women tonight, yep," I smile mischievously.

"Get her home safely. Please be careful, love you both. I'm going to be sad and single now." Sin pouts before turning on her feet toward her bedroom.

As always, Collins guides me down to his Tacoma with his hand entwined in mine, opening my door and slipping into the driver's seat. He drives us toward Downtown Tampa and Lockout. He opts to park the car himself rather than paying for valet. His masculine scent wraps around me like his arm does as he pulls me into his side while we walk to the front doors of the club.

Collins guides me to the VIP entrance, where we quickly flash our IDs to the bouncer. As soon as we cross the threshold, we're immediately met with the smell of alcohol. Being that it's Friday night, the club is chock-full of bodies moving in time with the dance beat that overpowers all other sounds.

"Drinks then dancing?" Collins asks in my ear, his warm breath over my cool skin sending a shiver down my spine.

"Please."

Collins pushes his way to the bar with me in tow. I remain tucked close to his side to avoid being separated from him. He gently pushes me in front of him, boxing me in from behind once we reach the wet bar top.

"Tequila sunrise?" His body and voice are seemingly closer than before. All I can do is nod in response.

Once I've downed my drink with another in hand, Collins finishes his water, and we make our way to the busy dance floor. With alcohol flowing through my system, I find my body loose and ready to move. The song changes from a beat that would have me jumping up and down to something sensual and slow.

Collins is behind me as we push our way through the crowd. Then he suddenly stops, pulling my body into his. My back is plastered to his front, his hands firmly grasping at my hips, and his breath hitting the side of my face as we move to the music. My heartbeat picking up so much that I can feel it in my ears at the way that our bodies will be connected for the next few moments.

Sweat begins to trickle down my neck, and in a move that has my breath caught in my throat, Collins moves one hand from my hip to my lower abdomen.

"Is this okay?" He breathes in my ear, cooling the sweat on my neck.

"Mhhmm." That's all I can get out because if I say words, I might beg him to take me to the bathroom of this club and push his hands lower than they are right now.

"These little touches... are important, ya know?" His thumb slowly rubs at the skin between my top and jeans on my waist as he continues to move us to the beat—using his other hand to keep me firmly pressed against him.

"Very important." I sigh, leaning my head back against his shoulder and letting the beat take over. I swear I can feel his hard length against my ass, which has me pushing back against him. Collins groans, his hold on me becoming the slightest bit tighter and it spurs me on.

Before I can do something stupid, the music changes again to something more upbeat, and I'm spun to face Collins. His chest heaves as his eyes bore into mine, while everyone around us begins thrashing around to "Mr. Bright-side" by the Killers. Collins seems to shake himself out of his stupor before joining the crowd in screaming the lyrics.

We bounce back and forth between close, sensual dances and jumping around like dorks as the music changes in Lockout.

As it gets later in the night, my limbs become heavier. Collins doesn't drink, but he doesn't mind if others do so to help loosen my nerves. I've had a few more drinks that are starting to catch up to me.

Turning in his arms, I press my front to his, leaning up

on my tippy toes so he can hear me over the music. "I'm getting tired, can we go back to your place and cuddle?"

"That sounds nice. Let's go." Collins plants a kiss on the corner of my mouth, which catches me off guard considering we aren't around our friends. I'm too tipsy to care though. He guides me to the bar where he pays the tab, then out of the club where I find my place under his arm.

"I think you need to eat and hydrate first, though. Can you text Sin and tell her you aren't coming home?"

"Yes to all." I smile groggily at no one in particular before pulling my phone out.

HARLEY

Hi bestieeeee. I'm going Collins. He promisd chzburger and cudles.

SIN

You need to sleep tonight. No shenanigans, Tipsy Tammy. Have him text me when you guys get home, please. Love you!

I giggle. She always calls me Tipsy Tammy when I'm just on the verge of being drunk.

HARLEY

Love u

"In you go," Collins says, pulling the truck door open for me.

Chapter 6

I'm Not Him

Collins

Having Harley's body pressed against mine all night, swaying sensually to the music, was vastly different than the first night I met her at Lockout. When she was timid, but still spun in circles with me on the dancefloor until everyone but Dom, Nik, and Sin called it quits for the evening.

It would've been the perfect night until it happened. We're driving back to my place, Harley munching on her greasy burger and humming along happily to the music—when a small, silver car that sped through the red light as ours turned green, narrowly misses a direct impact on Harley's side of my Tacoma. His car instead made an impact on the back end of the truck because I sped up a little. I knew as soon as it happened what caused this, when the kid, no older than twenty-two, got out of his car—red and glossy-eyed, barely able to stand on his own.

Her panicked scream of my name, "Collins!" It takes

me right back to that night, just a terrified sixteen-year-old arriving at the scene of one of his worst nightmares with his parents. The sounds of sirens, officers trying to get us to look away from the crumpled jeep on the side of the road, and the smell of burning engine oil combined with the smell of alcohol on the man who took my brother away from me.

Trying to snap myself out of it proves harder than I thought it would be. I pull myself out of the car in stiff movements. Quickly calling 911 on my phone, reporting the scene of the incident as I make my way around to check on my girl.

"Sit the fuck down!" I yell at the kid. I don't know why he even got out of the car. He obeys immediately, making his way to the sidewalk, dropping his head into his hands.

Even faster than I called 911, I swing Harley's door open, the panic that was simmering in my blood now full-blown, sizzling, "Tell me you're okay."

"I'm... Okay. I think." Tears fall on her face as I take it in my hands, slowly moving her head around, inspecting her for injuries.

I must be scanning her body more thoroughly than she expected because her soft voice breaks through my fog, "Collins. Hey. Breathe. I'm right here. I'm okay."

When I don't respond, Harley tries again, "Collins, baby. You gotta calm down. I think you're having a panic attack."

That's when I realize that I'm breathing unsteadily, my hands shaking furiously as I grip Harley's face in my hands still. Approaching sirens tell me I need to get it together so I can talk to the emergency personnel.

I take one deep breath, briefly closing my eyes and

shaking away the thoughts of Jordan, "Stay here until an EMT checks you out, please."

The switch in my demeanor seems to throw Harley for a loop, but I need to know she's okay before she gets out of the truck. She just nods in confusion as I head over to the officer who arrived on the scene.

"Sir, were you the one who called 911?" The officer asks as I approach.

"Yes. My girlfriend and I were driving home from Lockout when we got T-boned by that kid as we were passing through the intersection on our green light." I gesture to the boy who still sits on the pavement, slightly swaying side to side.

"Have you been drinking?"

"Never, especially not when I need to get my girl home safe. She was drinking at the club, and *he* has multiple signs of being intoxicated. He could barely stand when he unfolded himself from the front seat." I look back to see that an EMT has moved Harley to the back of an ambulance and is looking her over.

"Do you need to be checked out?" The EMT, Mari, I think she said her name was, asks me. The fog of adrenaline still surrounds me.

"I don't think so, but I'll go with her to the ER when the time comes." Mari nods before continuing to inspect my girl.

"I'm going to need to talk to them both. Go on and get your license and registration for me, call your insurance so we can get these cars out of here too." The officer approaches again and directs.

"Yes, sir." I head back toward my Tacoma, grabbing

everything we'll need out of the truck and head toward Harley.

"Is she okay?" I ask Mari as I approach, my fear that she has some sort of injury I missed seeping back toward the surface.

"Yep! She did hit her head on the seat when you had to slam the car to a stop, so we want to do a CT scan at Tampa Hospital as a precaution. She doesn't have any signs of a concussion, though."

"Thank God." I look toward the sky, blinking back emotion. Harley's hand grabs mine from where she sits, pulling me into the space Mari has vacated.

"Once the officers give an all-clear, we'll head over to the hospital." Mari tosses toward us as she passes by to check out the other driver.

"Collins..."

I steel myself, knowing that sooner rather than later I'm going to have to explain why I reacted that way. I don't know if I can do that tonight though, my emotions are running high and the adrenaline is starting to wear off.

Harley tugs on my hand, attempting to get my attention again.

"Harls... I can't." Hurt quickly flashes across her face, and I want to tell her it's not her, that I want to tell her about Jordan. That he would've adored her, probably tried to steal her from me. "I want to. I just can't, not tonight. I'm sorry."

"O-okay." Her voice shaky, I imagine the adrenaline is wearing off for her, too. That her body is tired, and the fear that she was previously feeling is rushing back in.

I sit down on the back of the ambulance with her,

pulling her into my arms. Letting her presence soothe my aching chest while mine hopefully calms her down.

"You two ready to get checked out?" Mari asks, coming back toward us.

"Let's get out of here," I say to Mari as I stand, she gets us situated in the back, then her partner begins the drive toward Tampa Hospital.

We call Sin on the way there, telling her we're fine but going to need a ride back to my place. I don't think she calms until she lays her eyes on us in the waiting room after we've been cleared to leave with orders to rest and relax for a few days.

"Are you sure you don't want to come home tonight?" Sin asks Harley for the thirtieth time as we approach the driveway of my home.

"I want to be with Collins tonight." She pauses, squeezing my hand reassuringly from the front seat. "I'll text you when we wake up, that we survived the night. I appreciate you coming to get us."

"Okay, love you both. Get some rest, stay hydrated." Sin gives us both a pointed glare before we exit the car. I carry our bags, unlocking the front door, and we're greeted by displeased purrs from Precious.

"Sorry, Precious. We had some unforeseen events come up tonight. Ready for bed, sweet lady?" Harls asks, scooping my cat off the floor as we head toward my bedroom.

"You can shower first." I assert, setting our bags on the ground. Harley drops Precious onto the bed before grabbing her duffle and locking herself in the bathroom without a word.

I find myself pulling out my phone and scrolling

through old pictures, wishing that my brother were here today. That his death didn't happen, that we were falling in love together, and that our parents wouldn't look at me and only see the son they lost. I was at his pro soccer games while he came to my hockey ones. The pain in my chest intensifies, and my eyes clog with tears. This time, I let them fall, knowing that I have a few minutes before Harley rejoins me. Once I hear the shower click off, I wipe away the tears and gather my clothes.

We pass each other silently as I enter and she exits. I quickly wash off, brush my teeth, and then enter the dark and quiet bedroom. The bed dips as I lie down beside Harley, she doesn't say anything, but I know she's not sleeping, the lack of her quiet snores and Precious' contented purring is telling enough.

"Harls..." I say quietly in the dark.

"Yeah?" She whispers back.

"I just want to hold you tonight. Tomorrow we can talk, okay? We both need rest."

"Okay." With her confirmation, I wrap my arm around her middle, pulling her into my side. She adjusts her head on my chest before throwing her leg over mine. We lie like this until we succumb to sleep.

I'm suddenly jerked awake by my phone vibrating repeatedly on my nightstand. I check to make sure my movement didn't frighten Harley, seeing that she turned over in the night, her shoulders slowly rising and falling. I grab my phone to see who's disturbing me at the ungodly hour of two PM. Oof, last night took it out of us. All of the guys have called at least twice and I can't bring myself to get up yet, so I text them instead.

COLLINS

I'm alive, and yes we're okay. No, I don't want to talk about it. I just woke up and we're exhausted.

They know I lost my brother when I was younger, but they don't know how. Although I imagine my lack of drinking says enough.

DOM

Dude. I thought you were dead. You never sleep this late, Sin told us y'all were fine but needed to see it for myself.

COLLINS

It wasn't as bad as it seems.

TATUM

Your car is totaled, bro. That's bad.

COLLINS

It's only totaled because I sped up to avoid Harley getting a direct hit.

MAV

Can we do anything?

NIK

I can make food.

Nik's always the first to offer food as his way of helping in any sort of situation. I appreciate him for that.

COLLINS

No. We're just going to rest today. I appreciate it. Someone tell the girls, Harley's still sleeping. I don't want them waking her up.

MAV

On it.

TATUM

Let us know if you need anything.

DOM

Seriously. Anything at all.

COLLINS

Thank you. Appreciate you guys.

I set my phone down and let my eyes drift closed again before I'm woken up by Precious. She's making biscuits on my back, I must've flipped over after I fell back asleep. She has an automatic feeder and litter box, so she's waking me up for attention.

"Morning, Precious," I mumble into my pillow. She moves away so I can flip to my side. Except something's not right. Harley isn't asleep beside me, and when I turn toward the bathroom, the door is open, lights off. I quickly stand up, exiting the bedroom.

"Harley?" I shout into the house.

"Kitchen." She hollers back. Oh, thank God, she didn't leave.

Stepping into the kitchen, I see what appears to be a roast, cornbread, and fresh chocolate chip cookies spread across the island.

"What's this?" I ask, hoping she didn't get up and cook us food after what happened last night.

"Guys dropped it off, maybe twenty minutes ago. I was going to come and wake you to eat soon."

"What time is it?" I groggily wipe my eyes.

"Six-thirty. I got up around five-thirty. I was exhausted."

"Same. Now I'm hungry."

"Me too." She laughs lightly but stops herself. "We need to talk."

"I know, food first."

We quickly plate some food, eating in silence on my couch. Only the sounds of our forks hitting our bowls and Precious' footsteps make sounds around us. As we sit here, I wonder where I should start. The girls don't know about Jordan. I asked the team to keep it to themselves, including their wives.

After we clean up from dinner, I guide Harley out onto my back porch, which opens into a modest yard. I've got a few wicker chairs, a small fire pit, and a shed out here. Nothing extravagant, just enough for me to come and sit on nice nights. We take chairs sitting opposite each other, and Harley sits there, waiting for me to talk.

I gulp in a heavy breath toward the ground before speaking, "I had a twin brother."

I dare to look up at Harley, and to my surprise, her expression has remained indifferent. I guess going to school for counseling will teach you that. I continue, "When we were sixteen, we had been invited to a friend's sixteenth birthday party on a Friday evening. I didn't go because I had a hockey game, so Mom took me while Dad stayed at home. Jordan—that was my brother's name—went to the party without me, he took our shared bright yellow jeep. After my game, Mom brought me home, she fed me dinner, and I showered. We were all hanging out, watching a movie, and waiting for Jordan to get home. Our curfew was ten, and we always had to text one of our parents before heading home."

I take a moment because the next part is the hardest to get out, but I know I need to share this with Harley.

"Take your time, Collins." She says quietly.

"Around nine-thirty, Jordan let Mom and Dad know he was headed home. The party was about twenty minutes away. He wasn't home by ten, then Dad's phone started ringing, which was weird for a Friday night. It was our local Sheriff's office calling and asking my dad to meet them somewhere. The officer told Dad to leave Mom and me home, but with the way my dad was breathing and his attempts to hold back tears, we refused. I think we both knew..." I stop again, my throat closing up, eyes burning. I rub my sternum aggressively, trying to alleviate the returning hurt.

"I think we both knew that Jordan was in bad condition or gone." When I blink, tears begin to freely fall down my face, and I find myself choking on air.

"Collins, hey, breathe. You're okay." Harley's voice is closer now, her weight in my lap, hands gripping my face as she tries to calm me. I don't even recall making space for her there. "You don't have to tell me anymore if you don't want to. I'm sorry for pushing you."

I find myself wrapping my arms around her, leaning back into my chair, and taking deep, steadying breaths. For a few minutes, we just hold each other as I center myself back into this moment with her here.

"I—"

"You don't have to." She maintains.

"I want to. You need to understand why I reacted the way I did last night. Thank you for giving me a minute to collect myself."

"I'm right here, and you can pause whenever you need to." Her hand rubs reassuring circles on my arm.

"Dad drove us to the scene. We all hopped out of the car, and what we saw... I wouldn't wish that on anyone, Harls. The jeep was crumpled into a ball of metal, there was a flipped semi, engine oil mixed with the smells of gasoline and smoke. The man who took him away from us... He had been drinking on his route, and his semi demolished the jeep. It killed Jordan instantly, I guess I'm glad he didn't suffer. The man stood there, trying to apologize, but all I saw was red. If there hadn't been police to stop me, I would've put my fist into his face. I think they saw how angry I was before the sadness kicked in and pulled me away from him. I... Last night. It took me right back to that night. I thought I was going to lose my best friend all over again." I don't care that I just admitted so much to her; it feels like a ton of weight has been lifted off my chest. It feels secure and right to share this memory with Harley.

Harley takes in my words for a minute before speaking, "I'm so sorry you went through that. I can understand why you reacted the way you did last night. I was just really worried about you after... Well, all of it."

"I know, and I should've said something last night."

"No, you didn't owe me anything. I'm glad you felt safe enough to share that with me though." She leans further into me, letting our bodies relax into each other. "How are your parents?"

I breathe out, "Honestly, okay, I guess. I don't see them

much. When we lost Jordan, I think they lost two sons. They couldn't look at me without seeing him, and we autopiloted being a family until I moved out to start college. We talk now and again, but we aren't nearly as close."

"Do you miss them?"

"Yes and no. I think it opens up the wound of Jordan when I'm around them; they don't love me the same way they used to."

"Have you considered talking to them about it?" She asks, the counselor side of her beginning to show. It doesn't bother me. I haven't spoken to anyone about this since we did our grief counseling right after Jordan passed.

"I tried... Back when we had grief sessions as a family and I felt like my parents were parenting me robotically. It didn't necessarily change anything. Since then, it just hasn't felt worth it." I shrug it off, pain whirling in my chest.

After a quiet moment, I ask, "Will it always be this hard to talk about?"

Harley's hand has moved to my head, gently running her fingers through my curls as she speaks, "Do you want the mental health counselor answer or the Harley answer?"

"Hmm, mental health," I answer after pondering for a moment. I feel like I've gotten the Harley response. I wonder what sage advice she'll have next.

"So the mental health professional would tell you that grief looks different for everyone. That you can't focus on if it will get easier, they might even introduce you to the button theory."

"Tell me more about this button theory." Genuinely interested in the knowledge she's about to drop on me.

"Are you sure? You're opening a can of worms for me to

get on a soap box here." She chuckles, her hand still mind-lessly moving in my hair.

"One hundred percent. I want to know more about it."

I look up to see her eyes light up just a bit before she starts talking, "Sorry, I'm not excited to have to talk about grief with you. Benji was never interested in hearing about my schooling or work, so it's just nice... I guess to be able to talk about it and have someone who wants to listen."

"I'm not him." It slips out so fast, her touch faltering for a moment.

"I know you aren't. So, anyway the button theory, imagine that grief is a box, and within that box is a button and a ball. The button never moves. When you first experience grief, the ball takes up the entire box, constantly pushing the pain button. As time passes, the ball shrinks in size, but it's always going to be there. It will just push the pain button less frequently—it has no rhyme or reason. It could happen while you're eating a bowl of cereal, or it could be triggered by a memory. The grief never leaves, it *might* get easier to talk about, but it's still there."

I stare at her, awestruck, for a moment. Taking in her round cheekbones, full, pouty lips, and hazel eyes as she waits for a response. Her beauty is radiant, but her brain does something else for me entirely.

"Thank you, that makes a lot of sense." I can't formulate any other response. My brain swirling with too many conflicting thoughts to carry this conversation. The one thing I do know is that I'm down way worse for Harley Wheeler than I initially thought.

Chapter 7

All For Us

Collins

It's been three weeks since the crash, but Harley looks beautiful as ever in the front seat of my brand-new Tacoma. Dominic took me to pick it up yesterday after I got a call that all of the auto insurance claims from our incident had been settled.

Harley sports black sweats, wearing a Manta Rays crewneck, and has a beanie secured over her head as we weave through the mountains. Red spruce and deep, green pines bracket the road we are on, leading up to the cabins. There's a light snowfall coating the ground and trees, giving the scenery a more dreamy vibe.

"It's so beautiful up here, and we haven't even made it to the cabins yet." Harley muses beside me. Precious in her carrier, purrs quietly as she sleeps beneath Harley's legs.

"It is. Are you more of a mountain or beach lady?"

"I love the mountains, I would come up here twice a year if I could. There's just something about breathing the fresh air up here that hits differently than it does in Florida." She answers, continuing to stare out the window, watching the world flit by.

I make a mental note that when I make her mine, *truly mine*—we'll be up here whenever she wants. Maybe even buy a cabin that can be rented out when it's not in use.

"I agree, everyone loves the beach. However, the sand in uncomfortable places and the unknown of what lies beneath the surface of the waves is none of my business." I tell her. The laugh that bubbles out of her has my face splitting into a grin. To hear her laugh for the rest of my life would be an honor.

"And it's like rubbing your skin with sandpaper as you wash it off." She says in disgust that the statement causes us both to cringe.

We continue our trek higher into the mountains and further into the trees, conversation continuing to flow between us. We take one final turn up a steep drive and are greeted by three cabins, everything dusted in a new layer of snow. The main cabin, which will hold the families, parents, Nik, and Dom, sits at the center of the land with a giant wrap-around porch and floor-to-ceiling windows looking out into the mountains. To the right sits a log cabin that I presume Grace, Jason, and Sin will stay in. To the left, down a small embankment, sits Harley and I's A-frame cabin. I turn my truck down the little driveway, slowly pushing us toward the cabin and into the flat parking area.

"This is so cute." Harley squeaks as I put the car into park.

"And it's all for us." Out of the corner of my eye, I see her cheeks pinken as she shies away from me.

"Let's get our stuff inside, and then we can join the others at the main cabin." She says, switching the topic of conversation. We hop out of the truck, Harley carrying Precious' carrier while I grab our bags. Harley uses the door code that Kodi shared with us in a group text, pushing the door into a mostly open floor plan. A small kitchenette sits to the right of the space, while a small, worn couch breaks the room in half, facing a small TV above a wood fireplace. Directly in front of us, stairs lead up to a loft space where our bed sits.

Harley sets the carrier down, unzipping the door. Precious mewls before slinking out and slowly taking in her new surroundings.

"I'll take these up," I tell Harley, sliding past her as Precious curls around my feet, purring happily at her newfound freedom. After taking the stairs up, I take in our sleeping space. A king bed covered in flannel sheets sits against a floor-to-ceiling window that looks out into the mountains away from the other cabins. To the right sits the bathroom, holding a shower-tub combo, sink, and toilet.

"Bathroom's up here." I holler down at Harley.

"Thanks! Coming down anytime soon? I'm sure that Sin and Dom are already making comments about us taking so long..."

"Sorry, the view up there is just unbelievable. I had to take it in for a moment." I say as I make my way back down the stairs.

"I can't blame you, I've been staring out this window while I was waiting." She gestures toward the sill where Precious has curled up. I quickly grab my phone, snapping a picture of my cat watching the snowfall.

"Let's go, Baby." I take her hand in mine, pulling her out of the front door and locking it behind us. We make our way up the small, built-in staircase, Harley in front of me in case she slips on the icy ground. When we reach the top, I wrap my arm around her shoulder, guiding her over to the main cabin just as Kodi and Maverick pull up.

"You go inside, I'll help Mav get the food and their bags." I pull her in for a quick kiss, sending her on her way.

"Go inside, Ko. Collins and I've got this." Maverick directs his wife once he opens her door and ensures she gets onto the snowy ground safely. Then, unbuckling and passing a sleeping Bella over to her. Harley waits patiently by the front of Mav's bronco for Kodi before they head into the main cabin.

"What can I help with?" I ask him after the girls have made their way inside.

"The trunk is stuffed full, and then we have a couple of bags in the back seat."

"You got it."

Once the kids are down for the night and the grandparents are handed monitors, ensuring that they can handle sleeping children, we all grab a drink, some blankets because we are Floridians after all, and head out to the porch where Nik starts up a fire in the built-in pit. The crackle of the fire is dimmed by the sounds of our friends chatting about the drive and plans for the trip. Harley sits in my lap, a mug of spiked hot chocolate in her hand, while her other hand absent-mindedly rubs circles on my bicep. My arms wrapped around her waist, her head tucked between my neck and shoulder. Around us, Kodi and Mav are in a similar position, while Darcy sits between Tatum's legs in a lounge chair, leaning into his chest, Conrad and Enid snuggled togetherin a chais while everyone else in individual seats. Mace disappeared into the cabin when we offered to let him hang out, claiming he had better things to do.

"You all are so in love, it's disgusting, actually." Sin groans from our left.

"If you wanted to cuddle, you just had to say so." Dom chuckles across the pit, opening his arms for her. All he gets in return is two middle fingers, making him laugh harder.

"So, we were thinking about driving down to the lodge tomorrow. There's some shopping, we can take Hayden and Bella to see Santa, grab lunch, and snowboard if the guys want to." Darcy says, sipping on her white wine.

"I want to be there when Hayden meets Santa, but also down to snowboard." Tatum says from behind her.

"Same," Maverick says.

"So, how about Santa, split up, then reunite for lunch?" Kodi suggests.

"Sounds good to me." Harley says, her typical mint smell mixed with the hot chocolate creates the most intoxicating aroma around us.

"I'm in if my girl is in," I add.

"If I'm up, I'll join. If not, I don't mind hanging here with Stu, Mom, and Dale." Sin shrugs, "I'm just not holding myself to early mornings while I'm on vacation."

"That's valid. I'm in." Dom adds.

"Same," Nik says.

"I'll text Grace and Jason since they decided to turn in early." Maverick throws out, quickly sending a text, then repocketing his phone.

"Do we have plans yet for the morning of Christmas?" Maverick asks his wife.

"Yes! Everyone has their pajamas, and we're planning a big breakfast for everyone with the chef of the group. Then we can do presents and just hang out, enjoy a white Christmas." Kodi's smile is so wide, it might break her face.

"I can't wait to see the kids' faces that morning." Darcy chimes in, I can't blame her, it's Hayden's first Christmas, and even though he won't remember it, she and Tatum will.

Quiet chatter continues about Christmas morning, and the rest of the evening passes in quiet tranquility. The guys and myself talking about which hills we want to try tomorrow. All the while, the girl of my dreams snuggles tipsily into my chest until she starts snoring, and I decide to take her back to the cabin.

Chapter 8

Mayo

Harley

Waking up the next morning, there's a heavy weight on my chest, and my eyes feel heavy, causing a slight panic. After forcing my eyes open, I find Precious curled on top of me, along with Collins' arm draped across my middle. I groan attempting to move my body a bit causing Collins to stir beside me.

"Morning." He grumbles into the side of my neck, the warmth of his breath causing a shiver to run down my spine.

"Good morning. We need to get up and ready for the day."

"Nooooo. What time is it?" One thing I've learned about Collins is that if he didn't have morning skates and early flights, he would sleep in every day.

Reaching over for my phone, I check the time, "8:00 AM and we have to meet everyone at the main cabin around 9:00. You can sleep a little more if you'd like, but I need to shower and eat before we head out, so you and Precious will have to cuddle."

"If you must leave, I will cuddle my Precious." He says her name in his version of Gollum's low, raspy, guttural tone.

"Oh God." I've never heard him do that before, and the laugh that escapes me is very unladylike.

"What?" He furrows his brows in offense, "You don't like my voice?"

"That was downright terrifying."

"Oh, come here." He brings the voice back, pulling my body into his further while whispering in my ear, "We forgot the taste of bread."

"Collins! Stop it!" I attempt to wiggle away again, laughing at his antics.

Rather than saying anything, Collins just holds me for a few minutes before allowing me up to get ready for the day.

"That was a fucking disaster," Darcy says as she attempts to soothe an inconsolable Hayden.

"You could say that again." Kodi responds, holding a tearful Bella to her chest, "Bella, it's okay, baby. We are far away from Santa now, and he has to go back to the North Pole soon to get your presents ready."

"I don't like Santa, Mama." Bella sobs. I've never witnessed a child meeting Santa for the first time, but Hayden immediately sobbing then Bella breaking out into tears when she saw him freaking out as they were set in his lap was not on my bingo card for today.

"You know if I were set into an old mans lap without my permission I would also break out into tears." Sin whispers under her breath, and I cover my laugh with a cough as our Mom friends shoot daggers at us.

"I know, how about we go and find a Christmas present for Grandma just from you?" Kodi offers her daughter.

"Okay." Bella finally relaxes a little as we head into the quaint little shop next to the lodge. I've got everyone's Christmas presents ready to go, but it never hurts to shop around a little more. One of my favorite parts of this holiday is the joy that the smallest gift can put on someone's face, the way that you remember the most minute detail about something they enjoy can turn their whole day around.

"Harls!" Sin calls me over from where I was looking at postcards to a small stand filled with local hot sauces. "Do you think that Dom would like one of these?"

"Dom, huh?" I tease, throwing my arms over my chest. And for the first time I think ever, my best friend turns beet red, trying to hide it behind her hair.

"Yep." She emphasizes by popping the p, "I just forgot to get him something, is all. I have gifts for everyone else, even Stu."

"Mhmmm. I'll buy it for now. The man puts hot sauce on everything, so I think this is a great choice, and then maybe a souvenir from the trip, like an ornament or snowglobe."

We stand there for a moment, looking over the different hot sauce options, before my eyes land on *the* one. It's a blend of blueberry and habanero flavors, donning a redheaded woman dressed like a sailor. The icing on the cake is that it's called "The Sweetest Sin", quickly grabbing it, I shove it into Sinclair's hands.

"Oh absolutely not!" She whisper-shouts.

"Come on! You can make it a joke, say something like 'the only sin you'll ever be getting from me'. The man would keel over. Wouldn't he, Enid?" I push while dragging Enid into our conversation and she somehow turns even more red, making me wonder if, just like myself, she's hiding something. We'll have to unpack that later.

"He definitely would love it. I vote yes." Enid chuckles maniacally, a sound I didn't think I'd ever hear come from her.

She ponders for a moment before saying, "Ah fuck it. The guy will probably love it anyways."

"I know he will."

"Auntie Harley! Look what I picked out for Grandma!" Bella's voice echoes throughout the shop as she approaches, holding an ornate, wooden ornament with a cutout for a photo inside. "We're going to put a picture of me, Mama, and Daddy in it."

"I think she'll love it, Bella." I smile down at my niece, pride at herself shining through her toothy grin.

"Bella, let's go pay so we can go meet Daddy and your Uncles for lunch." Kodi redirects her to the register, Sin and I following close behind with the hot sauce.

We meet the guys at the front entrance of Elk's Garage, and everyone greets each other. Collins beelines it for me, whisking me into the air and gently placing a kiss on my lips.

"Miss me?" I tease.

"Always." He says with all seriousness before placing me down and taking my hand in his.

Nik checks us in and then we are guided to the largest table in the restaurant. Collins sits to my right—pulling my chair as close to his as humanly possible, and Sinclair to my left, we sip on water as we all casually peruse the menu.

"How was snowboarding?" I ask all of the men.

"Epic," Dominic says exuberantly and much louder than the tone of the establishment we currently sit in.

"What an adrenaline rush!" Conrad whoops.

"I had a blast, but it was fucking cold up there." Maverick chimes in.

"You guys skate..." Darcy starts.

"On ice...." Sin chides.

"For a living..." Kodi teases.

This earns some pointed glares and muffled curses from the guys, but they know it's all in good fun.

"I saw some deer from the lift. You would've loved it." Collins adds from beside me.

"I wish you could ride the lift without boarding down the mountain. That would've been a sight to behold." I grouch.

"Hello, I'm Leigh. I'll be your waitress today. Can I get you started with some beverages or appetizers?" A petite, college aged girl interrupts from behind Bella.

We all put in orders for waters and assorted beverages

while Tatum orders mozzarella sticks and spinach artichoke dip for the table. Giving our thanks, the waitress walks away, and we resume our conversation.

"What do you think you're going to order?" I ask Collins below the rest of the conversation taking place around us.

"I'm thinking a burger and fries."

"What sauce?" I quirk an eyebrow knowing the answer but hoping he'll change his mind.

"Mayo." He flushes and Dominic immediately gags.

Time to play dirty, he's been doing it this whole trip—teasing me with touches and looks, calling me Baby, holding me close. Now it's my turn.

"If you keep dipping fries in mayo like a psychopath, I won't do the thing you like and refuse to watch the rest of Lord of the Rings with you, at minimum mix it with ketchup." Loud enough that the others clearly hear me, all heads turn to us.

"Oh shit," Nik mutters.

"Damn." Conrad adds.

"Got his ass." Mace chuckles while Enid smacks her younger brother and her boyfriends arms simultaneously.

"No, she didn't." Darcy squeaks.

"You wouldn't dare," Collins says, mouth hanging aghast.

"Oh, I would. Just try it..." I flutter my eyelids towards him, "for me."

"Ugh fine." He concedes. Small cheers of victory flit throughout the table that I might have finally broken this behavior that never should have started in the first place. "What are you eating?"

"French onion soup and chicken avocado club," I respond.

"That sounds delicious. Can I have a bite?" Sin asks from my other side.

"For you... always." I wink at my best friend. The waitress comes back by dropping off our appetizers and drinks. We order our meals and then we wait, it's surprisingly quick how fast they bring our food out, given it's the Christmas season and the slopes are packed outside.

"Give it a taste." I shove the perfected ratio of mayochup toward Collins, waiting with bated breath for him to give it a try. I've been making this mixture since I was a child and know exactly what amount to mix to give the perfect dipping sauce.

I watch as he grabs a fry, dunking it in, then bringing it up to those perfectly plump lips.

"Final verdict?" I ask once he's fully finished his bite.

"Eh. I didn't hate it." He shrugs and shock paints my features immediately.

"I'm kidding, Peppermint. It was delicious, I think this is my new favorite dipping sauce, but only if *you* make it." He winks casually at me before continuing to eat, and rather than focus on the flutter that happened in my lower belly at his wink, I dig into my food. Lunch goes by with continued stories of snowboarding, bullying the guys into stopping back into the lodge shop, and then back to the cabins to rest before family dinner.

Chapter 9

Quixotic

Collins

"Quixotic. That's going to be twenty-six points." Darcy smiles smugly from across the table in the main cabin.

"What does that even mean?" Dom grumbles, dropping his head into his hands.

"Unrealistic and impractical. Quixotic." Harley supplies before Darcy can answer.

"I told y'all that my woman would wipe y'all with this game," Tatum speaks as he walks by dropping a fresh glass of wine to his girlfriend.

"I mean she is the author of the group." I shrug.

"Words are hard for everyone, Collins. I don't think you understand how many words I have to google synonyms or definitions for when I'm writing." Darcy responds casually.

"Chili is just about ready." Dale's gruff voice carries from the kitchen area where he and Victoria have been working since earlier this afternoon.

"Smells great!" Kodi acknowledges from where she, Stu and Bella play Go Fish on the living area floor.

"It does, Mr. Dale," Bella adds excitedly.

Today has been a relaxed day, we all gathered late in the day for Dale's famous chili and all the fixin's prepped by Victoria. We've had Christmas music playing in the background while playing different board and card games, each of us taking turns playing something with Bella. Harley and I played about fifteen rounds of Hungry Hungry Hippo with her earlier today. Bella giggled the whole time, Harley smiling fondly at her each time she declared she won a round–even though there were a few rounds she didn't win.

"Alright, let's eat," Dale says about ten minutes later. We all plate up some food after cleaning up the pieces of our game.

"Everyone ready for Christmas?" Stu asks the table and receives a chorus of nods and mmms as we devour dinner.

"I cannot wait to spend the morning in our matching pajamas and eating breakfast casserole," Grace says. We learned that the recipe she uses is one that Rose, her and Mavericks mother used to make for them every Christmas morning. Stu's smile is soft yet you can see the sadness behind his eyes that his wife isn't here to experience this with him.

"I love how we are merging old and new traditions together," Maverick adds happily, pulling Kodi closer into his side.

If I wouldn't have found this family with my team and Kodi's friends then I don't know what my Christmases in Florida would look like. My parents don't really celebrate and I think they only did it after Jordan passed for me. I find myself squeezing Harley's hand gently under the table, a reassurance to myself that it may be time for me to share the hurt I've kept inside for years. As if she can read my mind, she squeezes mine back twice.

"I..." I start to speak, clearing my throat before feeling another squeeze around my fingers. "I have something that I'd like to share."

The weight of everyone's eyes turning to me—watching and waiting causes the pressure building in my chest to feel like it might explode.

"Go on." Harley encourages softly, just for me. "It's time they know, they love you."

"When I was a teen, I lost someone very important to me. It's the reason I don't drink to this day. Umm... I had a twin brother, Jordan, he was taken from us when we were sixteen because of a drunk driver. He was my best friend. I'm... I'm just really glad I have you all to spend the holidays with, I don't know what they would look like without you all. I'm sorry that I kept it from you guys." I can't bring myself to rehash it the way I did with Harley after our accident but sharing—even just this much is a good step for me. It's a step in healing, in letting Jordan's passing be something that I can talk about, something that I don't need to hide from the people who care about me most. The people that I guarantee Jordan hand picked for me.

There's a moment of silence before Nik speaks, "I'm sorry that you've been holding onto that. Please know you can talk about him whenever you want, however much or little it is that you want to share."

Maverick adds, speaking to me but looking toward his sister and father, "Grief is a long and hard journey. Sometimes it hits us when we least expect it and we don't know how to express that to others. Including the ones we cherish most in the world."

"We're here for you, bro." Dom pats me on the shoulder from my side.

"I really don't know why I spit all of that out right now." The dam holding back my watery eyes threatening to break.

"Because you wish he was here and even though he's not, you've found other brothers in your team," Harley speaks with her almighty wisdom.

"Amen." The guys say in unison. No one looks at me with pity in their eyes as I wipe my tears away, no one offers me condolences or shames me for not sharing this with them sooner. All I feel is the love and support from the people around me along with this lingering feeling that Jordan brought these people to me somehow.

Chapter 10

We're Stuck

Collins

I wake to the sounds of howling winds and shaking trees. Turning my phone over, I see that it's only 4:00 AM and entirely too early for me to be up. Groggily, I peer over Harley's body to see what's happening outside. I can't see farther than five feet from the window, fresh white snow layers everything and continues to come down heavily. The winds continue to hit the side of the cabin. Snowstorm... Fucking wonderful.

I huddle closer to Harley, laying my arm over her middle and attempt to fall back to sleep for a few hours. It takes a bit considering all the noise but it eventually lulls me back into a slumber.

"Holy shit." These are the words that wake me up for the second time today.

"What is it?" I grunt without opening my eyes to face the sun.

"It's snowing... Like a lot. You can't even see outside."

"Oh.. Yeah I know. We're probably going to be stuck here a few days."

"What! No! It's almost Christmas." Harley jumps from the bed, slipping her house shoes on and running downstairs towards the front door. I follow, at a much more relaxed pace than she was at to find her with her face pressed against the glass pane of the cabin door.

"The snow is almost to the window!"

"Yep, definitely staying in our pajamas today." I smile. Knowing I'll get a few days by myself with her has my heart fluttering with excitement, and my cock too. That could be because of the way her ass juts out as she leans into the front door trying to see outside.

Harley

"Ugh! I can't believe we're stuck." I groan, banging my head against the front door that we can't open at this point. Unless we want snow falling into the cabin.

"It'll be fine, Peppermint. We have food, games, each other, and The Lord of the Rings: Two Towers on streaming." Collins says from behind me, pulling my body away from the door and into his chest.

"I know but Nik was making chocolate chip pancakes. Plus day after tomorrow is Christmas Eve and if we can't make it up to the cabin, we missed the whole point of this trip–celebrating Christmas with our friends," I mumble into his chest.

"Hey," Collins places his finger beneath my chin, pulling my gaze up to his, "snow storms typically only last a day or two then we'll be able to shovel a path up to the main cabin. So today, you'll have to settle for spending extra time cuddled up to your boyfriend and Precious."

"Oh no, that sounds absolutely horrible." I accentuate the sarcasm in my voice with a long groan. Truthfully, being stuck inside with Collins all day kind of sounds like a dream come true.

"I know, we make the worst company." He smirks down at me. That smirk has me swaying on my feet to avoid rubbing my thighs together.

Before I know what's happening, Collins has thrown me over his shoulder and is carrying me toward the couch.

"Put me down, you big goof." I laugh, smacking his back.

"No need. Almost there." He lays me gently onto the couch before plopping down beside me, lifting my feet into his lap.

"Okay, so how do we want to start our day?" Collins adds.

"This... This is nice." I smile sheepishly. This couch while well-loved is so comfortable, that you can't help but let the cloud of cushion pull you in.

"Okay but what about breakfast? I don't have chocolate chip pancake ingredients but I do have eggs, bacon, avocado, some plastic cheese, and everything bagels. Oh and mayo."

"That sounds wonderful."

"You stay here, I'll make breakfast and coffee." He smiles before getting up and heading toward the kitchen. Precious takes up residence by my head after Collins walks away. While the sounds of Collins moving around the kitchen surround me, I decide to pull out my phone and check the girls' chat that includes Grace and Enid.

SIN

UGH, I can't believe we got snowed in.

HARLEY

I'm very upset about missing chocolate chip pancakes

Darcy then sends a photo of Hayden and Bella covered in melted chocolate and syrup, sideways smiles on both of their faces.

HARLEY

If they weren't so cute, I'd be mad at you for sending that.

DARCY

That's why I sent them and not my own plate.

KODI

We wish you all were here.

GRACE

If we could open the door, I would've braved the cold for food. But it's piled up.

HARLEY

Same.

ENID

Yeah, I can barely see your cabin from our bedroom window.

SIN

I can see the main cabin but past that it's just white.

HARLEY

I will say, the view from our bed is killer. I kind of want to take my book up there and spend the day reading with snow as my backdrop.

KODI

Ooo what're you reading?

HARLEY

Our very own Darcy's latest release.

DARCY

Be warned. Chapter thirteen may have you pouncing on ya man. At least that's what Kodi says.

GRACE

I second that.

SIN

I don't have a man, but hard agree.

ENID

Definitely. Conrad and I had a good night after I read that chapter. 😈

I giggle out loud and it causes Collins to pop his head over the couch asking, "What's so funny? Jesus, you're bright red."

"Just the girls being the girls. Continue as you were." I blow a kiss up at him which he catches and sticks in his pocket before turning back to the kitchen.

HARLEY

Thanks for the heads up. About to enjoy breakfast, talk later 🖤

Collins and I spend the rest of the day playing Scrabble, drinking hot chocolate, and watching The Two Towers. We take multiple pauses for refills and snacks along with Collins explaining how certain scenes were shot or the slightest differences from the books. He's always nerded out over this franchise and I can't blame him. I get the hype now. It's the perfect amount of fantasy storytelling blended with action and the smallest bit of romance.

On a yawn, I say, "Alright, I think I'm ready to shower and head to bed."

Collins holds me tighter from behind, "But we were so cozy."

"We can be cozy in bed in about twenty minutes." I try to wiggle free from his hold but he's got me tight. Well, that and the fact that I'm not *trying* that hard.

"Fine." He whines but unwraps himself from me.

"I'll be fast." I quickly peck his cheek, running upstairs, grabbing my toiletries and clothes then shutting myself into the bathroom. I bounce on my feet, waiting for the water to warm then decide to brush my teeth and wash my face instead of jumping around.

Once the water is hot enough to boil potatos, I pull my clothes off and step into the shower. Letting the heat warm my body for a moment before washing, rinsing, and repeating my way to feeling clean.

Stepping out of the shower, I quickly realize we threw the towels in the washer and dryer earlier today forgetting to bring them upstairs. *Fuck.*

I put as much of myself behind the door as possible before I peek my head out of the bathroom to find Collins leaning against the headboard in his jeans and deep red sweater. He looks up when he hears the door click open but quickly realizes I'm undressed and his gaze heats.

"We... uh... left the towels downstairs. I have an extra in my suitcase though if you would grab it for me. Please."

"Yep. Yes, I can do that for you." He quickly stands and speeds across the room to my bag, opening it, "where?"

"In the top half, should be just on top," I say, expecting him to grab my towel and be over here in a moment, but he hasn't made his way back yet. I can't crane my neck any further without exposing my chest.

"Collins, my suitcase isn't that big." I chuckle, hoping it will grab his attention.

"No, it's not." His voice sounds firmer, almost more gruff than it had a moment ago.

"Then... What's the holdup?"

Just as I'm about to swing the door open and go get the towel myself, Collins appears in front of me with... oh God. He's holding my towel in one hand and the black, silicone sex toy that Sinclair bought that I intentionally did not put in my suitcase for this trip in the other. The sneaky bitch must have slid it in there before we left, I'm going to have to murder my best friend.

My cheeks instantly heat but Collins isn't upset or even embarrassed. If anything, he looks turned on, ready to devour me whole. My pussy clenches at the thought and I feel emboldened to do something that I wouldn't normally feel confident enough to do. With Collins though, I feel desired, I feel like I can do anything and he'll watch with rapt attention. I push the door open, exposing my wet body, hair dripping down my back, nipples pointed from his stare, and the slight chill.

"Harley." He growls.

"Collins." I purr back.

"I'm going to give you a choice, and I want you to do whatever you're comfortable with."

"Okay."

"I can give you the towel and we can pretend that you're not standing naked in front of me tempting me to take you right here like I've dreamt about for almost two years. Or you can show me how you use this on yourself, Peppermint. I won't touch you unless you want me to." His chest rises and falls as he speaks, his eyes roaming over my body causing a chill to wrack through me.

I pause, considering if this is a line I'm ready to cross or not. He doesn't push as he waits for me to respond, he just stands there with wondering eyes. Ultimately, I know that in Collins' hands I'm safe. That if we start something and I don't want to finish it, I won't have to, which leads me to tell him, "I want to show you."

I stick my hand out for the toy, he hands it over then steps back a few feet giving me space to exit the room.

Taking the toy, I lower myself to the bed, letting my legs fall open for Collins. This whole interaction has desire building within me but I'm not quite ready to take the toy so I let my free hand roam my body. Down over my nipples, pinching and rolling each one between my fingers before bringing the vibrator to my clit.

"Use the remote Collins." He clicks the button once, an intense vibration begins against my clit.

"How does that feel?"

"I need more." I moan as he clicks the button again, the intensity ratchets up to a steady but perfect buzzing. "There, that's good."

"Show me what else you do when you want to feel good, Baby." He groans, scrubbing his hands down his face as he watches me move the toy away from my center, suctioning it to the hardwood floor and dropping to my knees above it. I tweak my nipples as I drop myself onto the toy slowly and then lift myself off. Collins groans as he watches me pleasure myself, his cock straining against his pants.

"Collins." I moan his name, wishing the feeling of fullness was coming from him instead.

"Yeah, Peppermint?" His eyes glued to the place where my pussy and the toy meet. Wetness dripping down it and onto the floor.

"Come closer and take your cock out. I want to see it." Within seconds, his jeans are off but he's still standing about a foot from me, giving me the space he knows I need which somehow makes me even wetter. The deep V of his stomach and light smattering of hair leads down to the most beautiful cock I've ever seen. It's smooth, long and holy shit. A piercing through the head of his cock that I imagine would touch all of the right places inside me.

"See something you like, Peppermint?" A mischievous grin spreads across his face as I continue taking him in.

"Does it hurt?" I pause my movement, inclining my head at the small metal bar with two bulbs on each end.

"Quite the opposite." Fuck me, where did this confidence come from.

"Touch yourself," I beg, almost whimpering. His hands work his cock slowly, his thumb swiping along the pierced tip, pulling a groan from him. His eyes never leave mine though, looking for some sign that I'm uncomfortable or want to stop. However I don't want to stop at all.

"I'm so close." I cry out.

"Me too, you are such a pretty picture riding that cock Baby. You'd look even prettier painted in my cum." His head falls backward and he begins to pull on his cock more aggressively. My breaths begin to come out shallow and rough, my movements on the dildo becoming choppy.

"Fuck, I'm coming," I scream. My pussy convulsing around the toy, wetness spilling out of me, legs shaking.

"Where Peppermint?" He moans, looking directly into my eyes.

"My chest." With one final pull, Collins's cum paints my chest in long ropes, dripping over my breasts and down my stomach as we both pant.

Collins steps closer, reaching down and rubbing his cum into my skin before swiping some up with his fingers, "Open."

He gently sticks his fingers into my mouth and I gladly suck them clean, letting his flavor explode across my tongue.

His dick twitches in front of my face causing me to squirm, as he notices a smirk forms across his face.

"You're so good for me. Let's get you cleaned up." He extends a hand, helping me off the ground.

I thought I was in deep before, but now I don't think I can go back.

Chapter 11

Take It Slow

Collins

Having Harley spread out, bouncing up and down on that toy was probably the hottest thing I've ever seen. I know she was putting herself in a vulnerable position which is why I stood back, hands clenched at my sides watching with rapt attention as she pleasured herself until she permitted me to come closer. Self-restraint is something I'd say I have loads of but when it comes to Harley Wheeler, I want to give into all of my deepest pleasures. I'll wait though until she's ready, one step at a time.

With all that she went through in her previous relationship, I know that aftercare—while always an important step, is going to be vital here if we want to take steps forward instead of backward.

"How did that feel?" I ask as she waits for the shower to warm in the room beside us.

"Shower first?" She asks, cheeks and chest heated red.

"Okay, I'll hop in once you're done." I can't help but lean in and place a chaste kiss on her forehead before she exits the room.

After our showers we're cuddled up in bed, my hand moving up and down her back, I ask again, "How was that for you?"

"Really fucking good." She pauses, "But I don't think I'm ready to do more... Yet."

"That's okay, we can go at your pace." I pause, "We don't have to do anything at all. Having you like this, it's all I need."

"Let's just take it slow, there's no rush right?"

"No rush at all, Peppermint." I let my lips find the top of her head, then her lips.

"Goodnight, Freckles." She whispers into the dark once we part.

"Night, Harley."

By Christmas Eve, the snow has finally relaxed into a flurry and we should be able to clear a path up to the main cabin in the morning. Harley has been stressing about if we'd make it to celebrate with our friends, but I feel confident that we'll all be together come tomorrow. Today though, I plan to keep her to myself for a little while longer.

TATUM

How's it looking down there, Collins?

COLLINS

Much better. I think we should be able to make it up tomorrow.

MAVERICK

Definitely. We can help clear a path on our end before everyone gets up.

COLLINS

Thanks, guys.

DOM

Hope you've enjoyed your alone time.

JASON

I know we have 😏

MAVERICK

That's my sister you're talking about.

JASON

Sorry, man.

NIK

While you guys lie in bed fooling around on your phones, I'm down here prepping the meals for tomorrow. Could use some help.

MAVERICK

It's like 8:00 AM, give a man a second to wake up.

DOM

We wake up at 5:00 AM most days for morning skates, I think you'll be okay. I'll be down in a second, just gotta put on some pants.

COLLINS

You guys have fun helping Nik. I'm going to hang out with my woman.

TATUM

Lucky you. I'll be down soon, Nik.

COLLINS

See you guys in the morning.

"What are the guys up to?" Harley asks, turning to my side and burrowing her head into my shoulder.

"Nik is prepping for tomorrow. Everyone else is in bed. Jason and Grace are enjoying their time snowed in."

"Poor Sin. Her headphones must be coming in handy."

"Can I ask you something?" I've been thinking about this since the other night, but I haven't brought it up.

"Go for it." She tosses back.

"Did you purposely pack the sex toy?" I'm not mad if she did, but also given the circumstances surrounding our "relationship" and knowing we were going to be sharing a bed, I can't imagine that she would've intentionally included it.

Her face flames bright red before she takes a deep breath and quickly responds, "Nope, I didn't. My *supposed best friend* thought that because we'd have so much alone time, a new toy would be useful for us. She gave it to me before our first date... I specifically left it in my drawer at home, but I guess when I was doing my last minute packing stuff she slipped it into my suitcase."

"That sounds like something she would do." I chuckle.

"Yep. Definitely, I'm still going to strangle her with the popcorn garland in the morning, and I'm returning her Christmas present for that."

Realistically, I shouldn't say what I'm thinking, but boldly I find myself murmuring in her ear, "Does she deserve to be strangled when we got so much pleasure out of our experience?"

There's a deafening silence surrounding us for a moment then I can't help but say, "I– I'm sorry. I shouldn't have said that."

"No. You're right, maybe I should let her live to see another day. I just haven't gotten used to how filthy your mouth is yet."

"Oh, you haven't seen anything yet, Harley."

Chapter 12

C+H

Harley

Luckily, the storm cleared up yesterday morning and now we sit around the kitchen table enjoying the breakfast spread that Nik and the guys prepped yesterday. A copycat of the Hart family breakfast casserole, assorted fruits, and a plethora of other foods make their way around the table. Bella has asked to open presents no less than ten times, she can't help it but to be excited. Everyone dons the matching pajamas with their families and partners. Dom, Sin, and Nik were gifted Grinch pajama sets by Kodi—Dom has not shut up about the fact that Sin had to match him today. Harley and I wear green flannel sets that are covered in cats wearing Santa hats.

Once everyone has finished eating, we've cleared the table and refilled our mugs of coffee or hot chocolate, photos have been taken in front of the tree, and now everyone has settled around the living area ready to open gifts.

Stu and Dale take up residence on each side of the tree,

ready to collect paper and pass around gifts. They get Bella and Hayden settled with a few first, their parents assisting them in beginning to pull off paper while we all watch as excitement spreads across their small faces. I don't think Hayden quite understands what's happening, but the crinkling noise of the wrapping paper is enough to make him happy.

"Collins! This one's from your girl!" Dom says, taking my meticulously wrapped gift from Dale and passing it to Collins, who sits behind me, arms wrapped around my middle. He carefully unwraps the box before pulling out his brand-new mug. He snorts as he takes in the Lord of the Cats: The Furrlowship of the Ring, each character turned into a cat.

"I love it." He sets it down beside us, pulling my face to his and kissing me softly for a moment. It feels good to have his lips against mine again, and I don't pull away—well, until someone coughs, interrupting our moment.

"I have something else to give you later as well," I whisper under my breath, not looking away from him because I don't think he'll want the others to see this gift.

"Oh?" He quirks an eyebrow at me, drawing Sin's attention from my side.

"Is it sexy?" She whispers.

"You shut your mouth. I'm still mad at you, so you don't get to know." I smirk at her, and Collins is suddenly tense behind me, followed by a very hard and long length poking into my back. I don't acknowledge it aloud, but I do wriggle around a little bit, causing his grip to tighten on me in an attempt to keep me still.

The moment is broken by choked and uncontrollable

laughter coming from Dominic. We all turn our heads, and sure enough, he's holding a small note and the bottle of hot sauce I helped Sin pick out for him.

"This is perfect, thank you." Dom directs toward Sin, sincerity lacing his tone as he speaks. Sin waves him off as if she doesn't care what he thinks. One thing about my best friend is that she cares, and the way her cheeks have pinkened gives her away.

"This is for you," Collins says, placing a medium-sized wrapped box in my lap. I quickly unwrap it and open it to find some of my favorite treats inside, but also... a skinny velvet box that causes my heart to squeeze and pick up speed in my chest. Quickly flipping the lid, I take in the silver necklace with a small locket attached to it—upon removing the locket, I open it to a photo of us on our first date at the drive-in. Flipping it over, I see C+H is engraved on the back in his handwriting. I run my fingers along the letters in awe.

"Wow," it's all I can say at first. I've never received such a beautiful gift from anyone, and my fake boyfriend putting this much effort into a gift for me solidifies the fact that I don't want this to be fake. I want Collins McKee to be mine. Truly and wholly mine. There's a lingering fear that this could end in disaster like it did with Benji though and that is what keeps me from pouring all of my feelings out at Collins' feet.

"Collins, this is beautiful. Thank you." I turn, smiling at him and placing a gentle kiss on his lips, "Help me put it on?"

He takes the necklace from me, and I turn back toward the room, all of my friends with soft smiles on their faces.

Encouraging and supportive of seeing this relationship bloom.

After finishing gifts and enjoying dinner together, everyone heads their separate ways. Collins and I are slowly walking back to our cabin. We take in the snow around us, the silence of the mountains, and the stars so clear in the sky.

"Harley," Collins stops us in the middle of the lawn.

"Yeah?" I ask, turning toward him.

"Thank you." Collins wraps his arms around me as we continue to take in the night sky.

"For what?"

"Everything. Being present for me, truly embracing our relationship, and the mug."

"Well, that's what girlfriends are for, right?" I crane my head to smile at him, gently running my hand along the locket secured around my neck. "I still have something for you, and it's freezing out here. Let's get inside."

Precious purrs happily as we step back into the cabin after leaving her alone all day. Collins gives her treats and a cat toy as her gift, while I grab the special gift for Collins from upstairs.

"So it's not sexy, but I wanted this to be just a moment for you." I smile at him as I settle in next to him on the couch.

Collins takes the box from me, gently unwrapping the paper and pulling the gift from its bubble wrap. I wring my hands as I wait for his reaction. Maybe I overstepped, maybe this isn't something that he wants, maybe I should have just gotten him socks or something. Then he sniffles, looking up at me with watery eyes.

"Harley, I don't know what to say." He continues to take in the suncatcher with a photo of him and Jordan from a hockey game that I found in his apartment imprinted into the glass. It's engraved with the words "Look for me in the sunshine for I am always with you."

Collins continues to run his fingers over the photo, an occasional tear being wiped from his eyes. I let him soak it in. I let him grieve. I don't try to talk to him. I know when he's ready, he'll turn his attention back to me.

"This was so thoughtful. I know that typically people say thank you for gifts, but that doesn't encompass the appreciation that I feel for you... And this right now." He says, carefully wrapping the suncatcher back up and sliding it into the box again before setting it onto the coffee table.

"You don't have to have the words. Thank you is enough." I smile softly at him.

"Where do you think I should put it?" He asks, opening his arms for me to slide into.

"I was thinking on the back porch. You get such good sunlight back there, it'll probably reflect the colors perfectly at sunset."

"That's what I was thinking, too. We'll have to test it out when we get back." He says into my hair. *We.* Will there be a we when we get back? I mean, we did say that we needed to make it last through the holidays for our friends to believe it.

"Yeah, we will. Want to watch the Grinch before bed?"

"Let's do it."

I don't last the whole movie, and I feel my body lifted off the couch and set into the bed. A blanket pulled over me before I feel Collins settle in behind me, placing a gentle kiss on my head before whispering into my hair, "This is the best Christmas I've had in a while. Thanks to you."

I'm not sure if these are words that were meant for me to hear, but my heart swells with pride at the words.

We begin our trek back to Florida tomorrow morning, so as a last hurrah we've gathered around the fire pit for the evening. Taking it easy but still making the best of our time together. Two people were sent to get more wood from the side of the main cabin and haven't made it back yet.

HARLEY

Ma'am. You can't bail on our last night in the mountains.

Much to my surprise, ten minutes later and she hasn't responded.

"I'm going to go check on them," I murmur to Collins so no one follows me away from the fire, and everyone seems pretty distracted by their conversations anyway.

"Okay." Collins kisses my cheek before I remove myself from between his legs.

"Be right back."

It's not a far walk from the main cabin's patio to the

small shed that's hidden around the corner but you can feel the temperature drop, the farther you get from the fire.

The fire, along with the string lights, gives off enough light to lead the way. Right before I turn the corner, I hear a deep, male groan and, "Sin, stop torturing me like this. Stop hiding from me."

"I'm not hiding, I told you it's not happening again." My best friend's voice whispers into the night, strained with what I can only imagine is want.

Those ten words have me stopping in my tracks, wondering what I'm about to walk into. My nosiness gets the better of me, sending me scurrying around the corner. I've seen Sinclair in some pretty compromised positions before, so this won't be the first time or even probably the last.

Holy shit. I have so many questions.

None other than Dominic Montez has my best friend pinned against the side of the cabin, one hand buried in her fiery, red hair and the other gripping her waist. They must not have heard me approach because they are deep in a stare-off. Neither is speaking, and both of their chests are rising and falling rapidly.

I clear my throat loud enough to break the spell, which sends Dominic jumping back, falling onto his ass in the snow. Sin's mouth drops open in shock, cheeks flamed red, and her hand quickly runs over her body and hair to smooth out the wrinkles.

"Um... We were just getting worried... And you weren't answering your phone." I defend why I was standing here like a Peeping Tom. "But... I can see I was interrupting something."

"No–" Sin starts, but I cut her off with my hand.

"We can talk about this later. And we *will* talk about this later." I pin my best friend with a stern stare, and she just nods as if she just got chewed out by her mother for missing curfew.

"For now, you get off the ground," I gesture toward Dom, who's still sitting, ass in the snow. He quickly stands, wiping the snow off of his body before I continue, "Let's get these logs back."

Dom hurries toward the shed door, pulling it open as I walk directly beside Sin, whisper-shouting, "What the fuck, Sin!?"

"I promise it's not what it looks like." Her words were short and contrite.

"I don't buy it." I'm echoing her words from a few weeks ago back to her.

"Well, it's a good thing I'm not selling then." She volleys back.

"Mhmm." I hum, choosing to leave it alone for now. However, she's not going to pretend this didn't happen. Not with me, at least.

Chapter 13

Our Fake Relationship

Collins

I turn the corner to the main cabin just as Dom, Sin, and Harley come around it with arms full of logs. Harley's eyebrows are in her hairline while Dom and Sin look like puppies who got chewing on something they weren't supposed to.

"I was thinking y'all got eaten by a bear with how long the three of you've been gone." I tease.

"Sorry, Dom slipped. We were just giving him a minute to recover." Sin says robotically, eyes downcast. Her typical boldness nowhere to be seen.

"Ouch. Let me carry those." I open my arms, and Dom passes the logs to me before we continue the trek toward the patio.

"What did I miss?" I nudge Dom in the side, speaking softly so Sin and Harley don't hear our conversation.

"Uh, nothing really." Dom's shoulders remain hunched.

"You know you can talk to me about anything, right?"

"Even if I made you promise not to tell Harley?" He asks.

"As long as it wouldn't negatively impact her, yes."

"Maybe when we get back to Florida." He shrugs, putting his mask of confidence back on before we return to the fire pit, dropping a few logs in.

"All good?" Nik's gruff voice carries over the flames.

"All good." Dom asserts, he doesn't say much for the rest of the night. I can't help but wonder what was happening by the shed.

I take my place back in the lounger, pulling Harley back in between my legs after she's topped off her hot chocolate. Her peppermint scent floods my nostrils as she lays her head back against me.

"Are you sure everything's okay?" I hum in her ear.

"I can't say anything because I don't know the full story. But yes. Or I mean I think?" Harley says just as quietly back.

"Ready to head home?" I change the topic, I know inevitably when she has more information, she'll spill the beans. Or vice versa.

"No, I like it out here. The calm, being with everyone... Being with you." I hope she's leaving out the part where she wants to keep exploring this connection that's come to the surface between us.

"I agree. Life's much slower here than in Tampa. It doesn't feel as rushed, like I can take a minute to breathe in and enjoy each moment, no matter how minute."

"These moments are the ones that I try to enjoy the most. The ones where we're all together, everyone healthy and happy. Basking in the adventures we're lucky enough to enjoy together. Most of us are in love." A soft smile graces her features as she speaks.

After eating one last breakfast spread, packing everyone up, and the girls doing their final checks of the cabins it's time to head out. Now Harley, Precious, and I are tucked into the truck and headed back to Florida. Music softly fills the cab as we pass by snow-covered trees and the occasional car heading up to the lodge.

The first few hours of the drive are filled with light conversation, reminiscing on our trip and planning for the New Years party that I'm hosting. Harley has decided that everything needs to be extravagant, so she can wear this new, sparkly dress she can't stop raving about. Along with suggesting that we should set up the spare room for Bella and Hayden to crash in so their parents can hang out until the ball drops.

A few hours into the drive, the plans for New Years Eve are ironed out, and she's texted the group chat before we find a comfortable silence as I continue our drive south.

"Thank you for doing this, it's been helping me." Harley's soft voice pipes up.

"This as in our relationship?"

"Our fake relationship." She clarifies, and disappointment consumes me but I can't let it show.

"Right. I forgot to ask earlier, but are you going to be my New Years kiss, Peppermint?"

"Hmmm..." Out of the corner of my eye, Harley taps her chin, "I'm not opposed to the idea."

"Opposed to the idea? Is kissing me that bad?" I fein hurt.

"No, it's not bad at all." Then, under her breath where she thinks I can't hear her she adds, "it's the best kiss I've ever experienced."

"Well, I guess I'll just have to make the next one better." I shrug nonchalantly as I speak.

When Harley doesn't respond, I let the conversation die and we go back to driving in a warm silence. Eventually, I look over to Harley, her eyes closed, chest rising and falling slowly as she rests.

As she sleeps peacefully in my passenger seat, I'm left with reeling thoughts, my thumb quietly rapping on the steering wheel. The closer we get to Florida leaves me wondering what happens next. Will she change her mind and suggest we continue our fake relationship after the holidays? Or better yet, will she decide that our relationship should be real after all? Do I get to keep having the time I've been hoping for with the girl of my dreams?

Chapter 14

Truth Bombs

Harley

"So you're telling me that you're fake-dating one of your friends and the man you have feelings for rather than pursuing something real with him?" My therapist, Violet, asks. Her eyes are boring into my soul, and when she puts it that way, it sounds ridiculous. Who am I kidding? It is ridiculous. I could very easily walk up to Collins and say, "Hey, I've been into you this whole time and want to pursue this, but like... Real." I'm sure he would love to hear those words from me, I don't miss the way he looks at me across the room, the way he touches me whenever he can, or the way he made sure I was okay even before we started this endeavor.

"Uh, yep." I wring my hands together in my lap, knowing she's about to lay some serious truth bombs on me. That's the kind of therapist Violet is and the kind I need. I tried them on like underwear until I found her.

"Harley." Violet waits for me to tell her exactly what I know she's about to say.

"Yes?" I give her my cheesiest smile.

"You know what I'm about to say. And I know you know because you sit in this chair at your office telling people similar things."

"Ugh, I know okay?" I throw myself back on her green, velvet couch dramatically. "If I can fake date him, then I should real date him if my feelings are real. But I'm scared, what if he turns out to be like Benji?"

"Has he ever threatened you? Laid his hands on you? Does he make you feel bad for not spending time with him?" Violet was by my side as I navigated my relationship with Benji and knows how Collins was the whole time.

"No, I feel the safest when I'm with Collins. He gives me space, he doesn't force me to do things or keep me locked away. He literally wouldn't hurt a fly. I've seen him rescue a spider from his cat." I chuckle as I remember him locking Precious in the bathroom as he ushered a spider into a jar with a piece of paper, setting it free in the bushes out front of his house.

"Hmm..." She hums decisively, "We have ten minutes and you have homework."

"Lay it on me."

"The next time you're with him, you're going to treat it like it's real. Give him the *real* feelings and the real actions. No pretending."

"Easy enough," I say like I haven't been doing that this whole time.

"You'll report back to me, right?" She eyes me over her pointed glasses.

"If I must." I sigh dramatically, and we laugh.

"See you next week, Harley."

"Thanks, Violet."

"Good morning!" I sing as I step into our living room.

"Why are you so happy?" Sin bemoans.

"It's New Years Eve and I get to spend it with my favorite people!" I smile at her cheerfully. I'm happy that I get to spend it with my friends. Last year I sat in Benji's room while he got drunk in the living room with his friends until he decided he wanted my attention. Attention that could be compared to a two-pump chump. I bet Collins isn't like that, I bet he takes care of his woman. I'm hoping to find out tonight.

"I suppose that is worthy of being happy."

"Okay, you and I need to chat, ma'am." I flop down next to her on the couch.

"There's nothing to talk about." She shrugs me off.

"Oh no. Nope. Not happening. You need to fess up."

"I have no idea what you're talking about," she deflects again.

"Dominic Montez had his hands all over you. I saw it with my own eyeballs. Which, if I recall, you've said you would rather die than let happen. Ever." I press her further.

"Let's blame it on loneliness and a lapse of judgment."

"Sinclair Mae!"

"Bitch, you did not just middle name me!" She shrieks.

"Oh, I did! You're lying to me, that is like so against best friend code," I whine.

"Harley, please don't push this."

"I heard you tell him it wasn't going to happen again. What isn't going to happen again?" I try again.

"Sex."

"SEX!" I scream.

"Jesus Harls! Tell the whole neighborhood why don't ya?"

"Sorry," I smile at her meekly.

"It happened one time forever ago, and it's *not* going to happen again." Sinclair asserts.

"If you say so. Why didn't you tell me?"

"Because I swore him to secrecy and told him I would chop his balls off if he ever told anyone. So I kept it to myself, pretended it didn't happen." My best friend smiles sweetly.

"May I have permission to ask one question?"

"One and that's it." She narrows her eyes at me.

"Was it at least good?"

"Very." She blushes and we break out into giggles before she decides she wants to nap before tonight.

"You almost ready?" Sin asks later that day, looking down at her phone, sitting propped against my headboard in a deceivingly short black pleather skirt with black tights underneath. Her top is mesh, and you can see her black bra underneath it. Black combat boots sit on the floor, ready to adorn her feet.

"How do I look?" I twirl for her after securing my locket around my neck. I wasn't kidding when I told Collins I wanted to dress up for New Years Eve. I've chosen a red, sparkly dress with a drooping neckline showing just enough cleavage. It sits right above mid-thigh and has a small slit on the right leg. I've let my curled hair fall around my shoulders, but have a hair tie in my overnight bag for later.

"Holy fuck, you are hot as hell!"

"Thank you." I give her a small curtsy because bowing will show my ass but I'm not uncomfortable in this outfit. I can't wait to see Collins' face when he sees me. He asked if he could see it beforehand, but I told him he'd like the surprise better.

"What shoes?" I ask, holding up a pair of black stilettos and a pair of sparkling heels that match my dress.

"The red. Everyone is going to simply pass away when they see you tonight."

"I could say the same for you!" I throw back as I clasp my shoes around my feet.

"Let's go celebrate the new year, Baby!" Sin grabs my hand and drags me out of the apartment and down to where she's apparently had an Uber waiting for us. The ride to Collins' place is quick, as we approach the front door, my body begins to heat with nervousness as I recall my homework from therapy. I run my hands down my dress and take a deep breath before knocking twice and then turning back to my best friend.

"You okay?" Sin asks.

"Yep, just nervous for his reaction." I fib.

"I don't think that's going to be a problem, turn around." Her feline smile spreads before she passes me and enters the home.

I follow her lead to be met with Collins' hungry gaze, he's not even trying to hide it and a smirk tilts his full lips when I squirm.

"You are incredible."

"Thank you." I don't let my eyes leave his as I speak. I find myself taking him in as well, black dress pants and one of those God-forsaken white button-ups rolled up to his elbow. His orange curls are messily styled atop his head. "You look pretty hot yourself."

Collins doesn't say anything, instead pulling my body to his and gently kissing my lips.

"Ready for a drink?" He asks as he guides me toward the kitchen.

"Maybe just one." I don't mention that I want to be clearheaded for later, that if anything happens between us, I want to remember every detail.

"One drink it is then. Wine or mixed?" He asks before everyone notices my arrival.

"Mixed. Vodka soda with lime." I smile at him just before Enid notices me and starts squealing about what a stunner I am.

It's edging closer to midnight, about twenty-five minutes to go. The kids are asleep and we're all lounging in the living area, sparkling cider, beer, and wine in hand, waiting for midnight to strike.

"Does anyone have any resolutions?" Kodi asks.

"Continue my healing journey." I'm the first to speak up, "with the help of you guys, therapy, and Collins."

Collins squeezes my thigh in appreciation from beside me.

"Get these two moved into my place," Conrad smirks toward Enid and Mace, who's not even paying attention to the conversation.

"Is it a resolution if it's already planned?" She elbows him in the side playfully.

"Wait, really?" Darcy asks excitedly.

"Yep, Enid and Mace are coming to live with me once their lease is up." Conrad smiles proudly. It took him a long time to get to this point. The point where he felt like his life was worth living, and that he had a support system that wanted him around. I wasn't sure how he would assimilate into our group, but these three have quickly become some of my favorite people.

"That's fantastic news! You know we've got all hands on deck when the time comes." Maverick claps a hand down on Conrad's shoulder.

"Thanks y'all." Conrad addresses the room.

"Five minutes left. I'm leaving before it gets too kissy in here." Mace groans, standing from the couch and walking toward the glass doors. As he slides the door closed, he adds, "Happy New Year."

"Come here." Collins stands, pulling me up with him and guiding me toward the entryway of the living room.

"Can't kiss me with everyone else around?" I ask as he

puts my back against the wall just outside of the living room, giving an illusion of privacy that doesn't exist.

"Not the way I want to." He inches closer to me, letting one hand find my waist and the other inch up my arm until it's behind my neck. Gently rubbing circles on my pulse point with his thumb.

Chapter 15

Happy New Year

Collins

"Oh." That's all Harley manages to say, her cheeks flushed in anticipation of what's to come.

"Oh, is right." From the living room, we hear the clock begin to tick down to midnight.

"Ten." I smile down at her, I can feel the hunger I have for her roaring within me.

"Nine." A sexy little smile pulls her lips as she looks up at me. Her hands find their way up my chest, then she pulls me the slightest bit closer by my collar.

"Eight." A tight squeeze of her hip, almost bruising.

"Seven." A teasing touch of our lips, barely a ghost.

"Six." A groan escapes me when she doesn't let me deepen that kiss.

"Five." My hand moving from her waist to her ass, pulling her against me. My cock hardens behind my slacks when I feel her dress ride up the slightest bit, only to discover bare skin.

"Four." A small moan leaves her mouth when I squeeze her bare ass.

"Three." The smallest cant of her hips toward my thigh.

"Two." I bring my face impossibly closer to hers, our foreheads touching as I stare into her lust-filled eyes.

"One." Another moment of taking each other in.

"Happy New Year!" The voices echo from around the house, but all I see is Harley Wheeler. She goes to speak, but I don't let her. I use the hand behind her neck to pull her lips to mine. This one isn't gentle like the others. This is a silent claim; it's rough and long. It's me capturing tiny whimpers as my tongue slips into her mouth and explores it. It's her gripping my collar as if I'm her lifeline and she can't breathe without me. It's me sending up a silent prayer that everyone leaves soon because I need her alone. Now.

When I finally bring myself to pull away, her chest is heaving, cheeks somehow even more flushed, and the cutest smile gracing her lips.

"Happy New Year, Collins."

"Happy New Year, Baby."

"The best kiss I've ever had," Harley whispers.

"That's how I really would've kissed you on our first date, Peppermint." She doesn't get to respond because Nik is calling us back into the living space for photos. I quickly check to make sure her makeup is okay and we smooth out our clothes before rounding the corner where everyone else remains.

"Good kiss?" Dom waggles his eyebrows at me as he

gestures to wipe the corner of my lips. I send him a wink and a silent thank you before wiping away her lipstick.

We cycle through each couple, girls and guys shots, and group shots before spending another hour chatting, and everyone heads out front to pile into cars and Ubers.

"Check in when you get home, please!" Harley hollers in the general direction of our friends. Her instructions are returned with a chorus of 'yes mom', 'you got it', and 'you've got my location'.

"They'll be fine," I tell her from my place behind her.

"I know, but it makes me feel better if they tell me they're fine." She responds as we watch taillights recede before stepping back into my home.

As soon as the lock clicks, the air changes from light and easy to heavy and tense. Harley stands against my front door, hands twiddling in front of her, pushing her cleavage out further. She sways slightly on her feet, I'm hoping it's to relieve some of the ache between her legs.

We both go to speak at the same time, and I gesture for her to go first.

"Collins, I want you to take me to bed." She sounds so sure of what she wants, but I'm planning to continue to check in with her throughout the night.

"Fuck, Harley. What am I going to do with you?" I scrub a hand down my face as I continue to take her in. Those heels are sure as shit staying on for at least round one.

She takes a few steps closer, biting her lip causing me to step back into the wall, "I told you already, you're going to take me to bed. I want you to show me what it's like to be yours."

"Are you sure?"

"More than sure."

In an instant, I've flipped our positions, lifting her so that her legs wrap around my waist. My cock is once again straining against my slacks and pushing into Harley's bare pussy–I can feel the warmth of her. My hands are tangled in her hair. My lips on hers, moving down her neck and onto her bare shoulders, as her hands move along my body frantically attempting to touch me anywhere and everywhere.

"Collins," she moans when I move my lips from her shoulders to her chest, licking the open space between her tits. She pulls her dress to the side to expose one of her caramel nipples so I can take it into my mouth.

"Mmm." I groan into her chest, beginning to swivel my hips and relieving some of the friction between us.

"Bed, please." She gasps when my teeth graze her nipple before I remove myself.

"Pit stop first." I smile deviously at her. I begin to move down the hallway. I deposit her onto the kitchen island before pushing her legs open and dropping to my knees.

"This couldn't wait until we were in the room?" She questions as she runs her fingers through my curls.

"Nope, don't worry, it won't be the last time I make you cum tonight, Baby."

Harley's eyes connect with mine as she looks down at me, and she pulls her dress over her head, revealing herself to me. In a move that surprises me, she brings herself to the edge of the counter, letting her thighs rest on my shoulders before dropping back onto her elbows.

"Don't get mad at me for checking in again," I bite her

inner thigh, causing her to jump. "But you're sure you want to do this?"

"I'm okay, I promise." She dips her chin in encouragement.

I don't need any more permission than that before I dive into her center. The first swipe of my tongue through her wetness has us both moaning in pleasure. I can feel Harley's body beginning to relax, enjoying the way that I circle her clit, her legs falling further open, her eyes closed, and her mouth dropped open as she watches me devour her. Moving my hand up her leg, I gently push a finger into her, pumping in and out. Her hips begin to move in time with me as her moans become louder and her pussy begins to clamp around my fingers.

"Are you going to cum for me?"

"God, I'm so close. More, Collins," she gasps out.

I add another finger, rubbing that place inside her, and return my attention back to her clit.

"Collins, fuck, Collins!" Her moans crescendo along with the movement of her hips until she's clamping down on my fingers, and her thighs are squeezing my head. I don't stop until she's finished riding out her orgasm, her body relaxed onto the countertop.

I pull myself off the floor, leaning over her body, where she smiles lazily up at me.

"That was..." I don't let her finish, bringing my lips down to hers, her tongue flicks out, tasting herself on my lips. The little whimper that leaves her lips has me pushing my hips forward.

"I know." I pull her up, setting her down and guiding her to my bedroom. Opening the door, I find Precious curled in the middle of the bed. Much to her chagrin, I set her outside before closing the door behind me.

"You have too many clothes on." Harley points out before stepping forward and fiddling with the button on my pants. She lets my pants hit the ground before rubbing her hand over my cock, causing my head to drop back.

"Let's fix that then." I smile, letting her continue her perusal as I work on the buttons on my shirt. Once my shirt is off, she puts her hands into the waistband of my boxers, finding the tip of my cock and rubbing the piercing, eliciting a feral noise in the back of my throat. I gently walk her backward until she meets the edge of my bed.

"Lie back for me, Peppermint." Harley makes herself comfortable at the head of my bed while I pull my boxers off. I make my way toward her, stroking my cock, her eyes glued to the movement.

"Let me." I position myself between her legs, and her tiny hand takes over where mine was. The feel of her smooth skin against my shaft has me bucking into her hand, precum dripping from the tip. She swipes her thumb across it before bringing it to her mouth, seductively sucking it in.

"Fuck, Harls." She continues moving her finger in and out of her mouth before I'm wrenching it away and replacing it with my tongue.

Leaned over her like this, my cock rests at her slick center and I begin rubbing myself against her. My piercing is knocking with her clit as Harley sucks on my tongue.

"Can you come like this, Baby? Can you give me one more before I bury myself in this pretty pussy?" I break our kiss, moving my lips down her jaw, her neck, nipping and biting back down to those perky tits.

She nods frantically as her hands dig into my back and she meets my movements. It's not long before she's crying out my name again. It takes everything in me to keep from coming on her stomach.

"Are you ready?" I ask again just to be sure, foreplay and penetration are totally different ball games.

"Please."

I reach over to my nightstand, grabbing a condom before lining myself up with her entrance and letting myself rest on my forearms so I can look at her face. My eyes remain trained on hers to make sure she's okay. She twinges slightly when I push my head in, but nods for me to continue.

Once I'm fully seated, I give her a minute to adjust to my cock, and she wiggles a little beneath me. I look to the place where we're connected as I pull out and push back in again a few times. The feeling of her wrapped around me is unreal. When I look back up at her, she has tears in her eyes and I go to pull out completely, but she stops me.

"Collins, I'm okay. It's okay." She says as I still inside her for the first time. Kissing me deeply and adding, "I want this, I want you."

"You can tell me if it's too much," I respond in all seriousness but I can't help but to thrust my hips into her, eliciting her mouth to drop open.

"I know. Fuck, your piercing, it's so good." She moans, "Do that again."

I move my hips in the same motion, and she moans again.

"You like that?" I growl, and she nods her head fervently. Pushing up onto my haunches, I bring her legs up to her chest, lifting her ass off the bed a little bit, and this time I feel my piercing hit her G-spot. *Bingo.* She gasps, and I lose control. My hips rocking in and out of her rapidly.

"God, Harley. You were made for me."

"Yes." She chants repeatedly.

"You." *Thrust.* "Are." *Thrust.* "Mine." *Thrust.*

"Yours." She cries out as her legs begin shaking in my hold, and electricity tickles at the base of my spine.

"Rub your clit. Give me one more."

Harley follows my direction, her hand snaking between her legs where she rubs tight circles, her head falling back further, and her mouth falling open on a silent scream. Her pussy tightening around my cock, along with the way her chest arches off the best sends me over the edge, grunting her name as I cum.

Gently pulling out, she moans a little, and I set her legs back down onto the bed. Before disposing of the condom, and coming back with a wet rag to clean her up.

"Up," I demand.

"I don't wanna." She groans, shaking her head on my pillows.

"I know, but sleeping in those heels is probably not comfortable and I don't want to be the reason you get a UTI. Especially because I'm not done with you."

"Fine." She peeks at me through her eyelids before sticking her hands out for me to help her up. While she uses the restroom, I stride to the kitchen, grabbing water, ibuprofen just in case, and letting Precious back into the room.

Stepping back into my room, I find Harley still naked, wrapped in my sheets, her curls spread beneath her hair, and her body relaxed. I set her water down before joining, pulling her into my side.

"How are you feeling after that?" I ponder, I need to know I didn't push for too much.

"That was so good."

"I didn't do too much?" Her hand rubs small circles along my chest as I speak.

"No, you did everything right." She sighs contentedly. "I felt safe, cared for, and wanted. You did everything right. The orgasms were mind-blowing."

"I'm glad I could satisfy you." I chuckle.

"I didn't doubt that you would," she tells me softly, almost unsure.

I pull her chin up to me and kiss her softly before whispering, "I wasn't kidding when I said I wasn't done with you. Try and get some rest."

Chapter 16

Sweet, Angel Baby Collins

Harley

I woke up this morning with the most delicious ache between my legs. Collins wasn't kidding when he said he wasn't done with me last night. After sleeping for a bit, he woke me up for round two with his head between my legs again, then he took me softer and gentler than the first time. In round three, we were like rabid animals, claws and teeth, fast, rough, and urgent. I don't feel unsure about my decision to give myself to Collins last night. I feel like it was the best choice I could've made for myself.

Now I'm walking into Wake, Bake, Repeat for the yearly New Years Eve debrief with my best friends. We always ring in the New Year together, but what happens once we part ways is always a mystery until the next morning, when we're desperate for coffee and the will to live.

Walking in, I find Sin and Darcy already sitting at our

usual table in the back corner. Giant coffees sitting in front of them.

"You look like shit," I tell Sin where she sits with deep bags beneath her eyes and head resting in her hands.

"And you look freshly fucked." Darcy volleys back, no tact or even attempt to whisper that in this crowded coffee shop.

Darcy's words cause Sin's head to pop up, then she groans, "Fuck, I just gave myself whiplash. You are freshly fucked aren't you?"

I feel my face and neck heat as I remember the events of last night.

"Hello, my sweet friends!" Kodi's voice comes from behind me, delaying my interrogation... For now, at least.

"Let's go order our coffees, Ko." I drag her to the counter with me.

"Hey girls! Usuals?" Gigi, one of the regular baristas, asks as we approach.

"Yep!" I reply while Kodi orders the seasonal iced strawberry mocha. We pay, thank Gigi, and head to our table where she'll bring us our drinks.

"Okay, so who's spilling first?" Darcy prods.

"You." Sin raises a bright red, pointed nail in my direction.

"I..." I sputter, but Gigi rescues me by dropping off our drinks.

"You're going to tell us the truth about what's going on between you and Collins," Kodi demands.

"We let it slide for the holidays, but those are over, so... spill," Darcy adds, shrugging.

Here goes nothing, "I didn't want you guys worried

about me being alone on Christmas. Collins is a great guy, and I know you guys would approve. We fabricated a plan to get us through the holidays, and then we were going to go our separate ways. But... then he started acting like a real boyfriend, and he's so good, and I'm falling for him, and then last night..."

"Last night?" Sin waves her hand in a continuous motion.

"Last night he kissed me at midnight," I add, not sure how to tell them the next part. These are my best friends. Why is it so hard for me to admit that we had sex and I don't want our relationship to be fake? Maybe because I haven't even admitted it to him yet, and this confession could change the trajectory of us? Maybe because I'm a coward? Maybe because I don't want to be hurt again?

"Yes, we're aware. He dragged you off into a dark corner." Kodi laughs.

"Then you guys left and did whatever you did."

"Obviously banged in the New Year," Darcy states like it's common knowledge.

"Not me." Sin rolls her eyes, I narrow my gaze on her because after the incident with Dom in the mountains, I'm not so sure I believe that.

"Mav and I relived our bachelorette trip." Kodi smirks.

"Ew. We were there, the whole island heard you guys on that day bed." I gag.

"Anyways, what happened after we left? Collins didn't take his eyes off of you last night." Sinclair brings the topic back to me.

"So he kissed me again, ate me out on his kitchen counter, made me cum again without extra stimulation, and then fucked me not once, not twice, but three times." I spit out quietly. Three mouths hang agape around our table.

"Collins did?" Kodi asks.

"Like Collins McKee?" Sin adds.

"Our sweet, angel baby Collins..." Darcy exaggerates, then whispers, "is a freak?"

"I haven't even told you the best part." I giggle because my friends are rarely this shocked by my sexscapades.

"His cock is pierced," I add on conspiratorily.

"No." Kodi gasps.

"Fucking." Darcy adds.

"Way." Sin finishes.

I say smugly, "It was so good you guys."

"I will never look at him the same way again." Darcy says, her cheeks bright red from the information I just shared.

"And I can never eat off his counter again," Sinclair says brazenly and I give her my middle finger.

"Since all that's out of the way. Be truthful with us, then. Do you want more with him?" Kodi adds, eyeing me suspiciously.

"I think I do."

"Have you told him?" Ko asks.

"Obviously not! I can't do that."

"What? Why not?" Darcy asks.

"Because that makes it real."

"Versus what? Fake. Babes, it was never fake. Anybody could see that from a mile away, even if you guys were telling each other it was." Sin encourages.

"We only knew there was something else going on

because we know you. That after Benji, you weren't going to let someone in easily. Real or not." Darcy tacks on.

"Plus, he's had eyes on you... like forever?" Kodi adds.

"Just talk to him. I don't think it's going to end the way you think it might." Darcy tells me, placing her hand over mine. "He's not Benji."

"I know, and that's what's so scary. I know he won't hurt me and I know he'll take care of me. I know this could last." I sniffle, emotions clog at the back of my throat.

"I think you should tell him that. It's okay to be scared." Kodi validates the fear.

"Okay, I will," I say.

I leave Wake, Bake, Repeat with a renewed sense of confidence in letting Collins have every part of me. For real.

As I'm lying in bed that night, my phone begins to vibrate beside me. Seeing that it's Collins, I take a few calming breaths, hoping that I can maintain my composure and not spit out everything. I don't want to spill this information over the phone, and I won't be able to see him until they get back from their away game.

Pressing answer, "It's past my bedtime, ya know?"

"Yes, but I wanted to check in again after last night. Plus I'll be busy the next few days and wanted to hear your voice." Collins' soothing voice comes through the speaker.

"I'm okay. I promise, I wasn't lying when I told you that you did everything right." I reassure him. The way that he's made sure to check in every step of the way is just another reason that I'm ready to take the next step with him.

"Okay." He sighs into the phone, "I just needed to be sure. The highs after sex can blur the emotions, and I needed to know you're okay."

"I appreciate you checking in on me."

"Precious is excited to spend time with you this week."

"Oh, I bet. She's going to get so many treats."

"So you're the reason she's gaining weight," he teases.

"Maybe..."

"I'll miss you both. You'll be at my place when I get home?" He asks, slight hesitation in his voice.

"Is that what you want?"

"It is."

"Then yes, I will," I confirm.

"One more thing I wanted your opinion on." He sounds unsure of himself in this moment.

"Hit me with it."

"I was thinking about reaching out to my parents, inviting them to a game, or we could have dinner with them, maybe? They texted me over the holidays and I realized that maybe I should try. Not should, but that I want to." While I'm surprised that he's bringing this up, I'm not. I could see the internal battle he's been facing about not having his parents present in his life.

"If that's what you want, I support that entirely. I'll be there for you in whatever capacity you need."

"Thank you. I should probably get to sleep, early flight. Goodnight, Peppermint."

"Goodnight, Freckles."

Chapter 17

What A Game

Collins

"It's the beginning of the season. Now is the time to show everyone that the Rays are back and better than ever. Keep your head in the game, don't start any fights, and score some motherfucking goals." Nik shouts at us as we wait to skate out of the tunnel onto the Los Angeles Badgers' home ice. Hoots and hollers echo around the chamber before the music begins to boom, and Nik leads us onto the ice hopefully to our first victory of the season.

The energy from the boos, the cheers, and my team fueling me to make sure I help Maverick maintain ownership of the puck throughout the game as I skate out behind my teammates.

As we take our position on the ice, Mav looks toward Conrad, then myself to which Conrad sticks his tongue out, signaling Mav to move right. We learned last season that hand signals give us away, so collectively each line created signals telling us where to move. Conrad spends a lot of time studying our opposing team's moves and eighty percent of the time he knows which direction they'll move first if they get possession of the puck. Hopefully putting us at an advantage from the get-go.

The referee starts the face-off off and then it's off to the races. Hart and the Badgers center fight for possession before Hart fakes them out, sending everyone in my direction while the puck flies toward Hoyer. The Badgers head toward me, giving Hart and Hoyer an opportunity to gain some ground before they realize I don't have the puck. Montez hoots, and someone else cusses before I move into possession to protect Hart and the puck. Rogers isn't quick enough, though, because Hoyer passes the puck to Hart, and he sends it flying past the goalie's shoulder and into the net.

The rest of the game continues like this, fighting for the puck, fake outs, and close goals by both teams.

"What a game," Dom shouts as he sets a tray of beers and a water for me down at our table in the hole-in-the-wall bar we found to celebrate our win. All of us wanted to avoid the bars that would be swarming with Badgers and fans, except Dom who wanted to and I quote "get down".

"It was close, I'm exhausted." Mav sighs. I can't blame him, my quads are sore from chasing him down the ice, and I know for a fact he was moving faster and more than I was.

"Cheers to that." I chime in, clinking my water cup to his pint.

"I was on the edge of my seat the whole time," Tatum adds, he doesn't always travel with us for games, but since it's the beginning of the season and our first away stretch, he wanted to be present.

"You three pulled through for us." Conrad adds gesturing toward myself, Dom, and Mav.

"And I'll cheers to that." Nik hoots, raising his glass and drawing the attention of the other patrons in the bar.

"Alright, someone spill what's happening in everyone's lives." Dom suggests after everyone has gone back to minding their own business, "I feel like we haven't had dude talk since before the holidays, and I need to know what's going on!"

"Why don't you go first?" I ask, deciding to stir the pot, seeing if he'll bite about what happened with Sin at the cabin.

Dom thinks for a moment before shrugging, "I think aside from Nik, my life is the most boring here. I'm not doing anything or anyone exciting. Hockey's my focus right now."

I narrow my eyes at him but decide to leave it be for now, considering myself and Harley are the only ones that witnessed what happened... To my knowledge, at least.

"Nothing new here," Nik reports.

"Same. What about you, Collins? Anything new with Harley? You seem to be moving pretty quickly." Conrad questions.

"We're doing really well but I need to admit something." Now is probably the best time. I need opinions on where to go from here.

"Go ahead then." Maverick encourages, arms folded on the table in front of him.

"Harley and I technically weren't... Er aren't together."

I don't even know how to describe it, so I spill it all, "She was worried the girls would fuss over her too much on our trip after everything with Benji, and we both knew everyone wouldn't be surprised if we were dating. So... We dated or fake-dated I should say. Well it's never felt fake to me and I don't think it has to her either. We agreed to the holidays, and those are over but it hasn't stopped. I just don't know how to broach the topic with her."

I exhale a hefty breath after I finish ranting. Then I wait for someone, anyone, to say something.

"I fucking knew it. Fork it over." Conrad jabs Tatum in the side. I watch in confusion as Tatum slides one hundred bucks into Conrad's hands.

"What the fuck is that about?" Dom interrogates the two of them, completely ignoring everything I've just said.

"I told Tatum from the get-go, I didn't buy it." Conrad states smugly. "Not that I didn't buy you two having feelings for each other, but that I didn't think it was as organic as it seemed. I knew there was something else happening there."

"Now that you say that... It was suspiciously good timing." Nik ponders.

"We were just waiting for you to admit it." Tatum shrugs, "We're happy for you even if you lied to your best friends about it."

As I look around the table, I see my friends smiling toward me... Everyone except Dom whose eyebrows are scrunched and lips are pursed—similar to Hayden's before he starts screaming bloody murder.

"Whatever this is," I gesture vaguely at Dom, "... It's weird."

"I'm hurt." He huffs back at me.

"Why?"

"Because everyone but me knew what was happening between you two."

"No one knew though, they were guessing. The only people who had any actual context were Harley and I. You'll be okay, Bud."

Dominic hmpfhs before saying, "Is anyone else hiding anything from the group?"

I once again find myself narrowing my eyes at him and see the slightest pink form on his cheeks.

"Not necessarily hiding, but I do want to share something with you guys." Tatum's voice takes on a timid tone.

"Tell us." Maverick pats Tatum on the back.

"I think it's time for me to propose to Darcy. I've been working on myself, we've been working on our relationship, and Hayden's about to be one. I want her to have our last name." Tate says, his eyes watering slightly.

"That's so exciting, man!" Nik hoots.

"I'm thinking I'll do it at his birthday party. Everyone we love will be there, and I can involve Hayden. He probably won't remember, but one day we'll be able to tell him the story of how his Mama and I got engaged." Now tears fall slowly from his eyes as he speaks.

"Oh, I'm going to be a mess." Dom sighs, swiping at his eyes.

"Congrats, dude! She's going to be so excited." I chime in, a huge smile taking over my face.

"Not to steal your spotlight, but I also have news." Maverick cuts in, his smile huge but eyes swimming with emotion. "Kodi and I are expecting our next little one."

"What a night of great news! I know how much you've wanted this." Tatum says, returning Mavericks' excitement from earlier.

"But..." He emphasizes, "You *cannot* under any circumstances tell the girls. Kodi's going to tell them soon, and I want to give her this moment."

"You got it," I say immediately.

Dom mimes zipping his lips and throwing away the key. Nik nods in agreement while Conrad and Tatum promise to keep their mouths shut.

Chapter 18

I Said Sit

Harley

Today's the day. I promised Violet. I promised the girls. Most importantly, I promised myself that I would tell Collins how I feel about him when he gets home. That I would admit the not-so-fake feelings I have and would give myself over to him completely.

Now I pace back and forth in Collins' living room, Precious winding between my feet as I go. In the famous words of Eminem, "palms are sweaty, knees weak, arms are heavy" and something about his Mom's spaghetti.

I've prepped myself for this moment, making Sin listen to me drone on about what I would say to him. Unfortunately, the moment that Collins' front door clicks open I lose every thought that I prepared. Then, when his giant, green orbs lock onto me, a soft smile gracing his face as he takes me in from head to toe, I realize I'm going to have to wing it. I do the same, my gaze becoming stuck on the shape of his cock through his gray sweats that hang off his hips.

"Hey, Peppermint." His voice pulls me from the place I was stuck, and I feel my cheeks heat. Collins's smile grows as he speaks, closing the door, toeing off his sneakers, dropping his bags, and opening his arms for me.

"Hi, Collins," I say softly before jumping into his arms.

"I missed you." He murmurs into my hair.

"I missed you, too. Can we talk?" I ask, and his smile falls a bit as he puts me down. Rather than saying anything else, I grab his hand and lead him to the couch, where Precious makes herself comfortable in his lap.

"I actually wanted to talk to you, too."

"Oh." My eyes drop, the confidence immediately dissipating, and the anxiety that he's ready to end things between us increases.

"Hey, look at me." Collins encourages. "I promise it's nothing bad or at least I don't think it is."

"Okay, go on." I let my eyes come back up to his.

"I've been thinking a lot about us. I've been thinking about that first time I saw you walking into the club that night with your wild curls around your face. Like this one." He gently pulls at one hanging out of my bun, causing me to chuckle. "How on that night I told myself I would wait until you were willing to give me a chance, and I'd scoop it up. That I'd wait while you figured out whatever was happening with Benji. So when you came to me that day and asked me to be yours, even if it was supposed to be a ruse, I made another vow to myself. That now that I had you, I wouldn't let you go."

My heart stutters in my chest, I can't get the words out, but I know that I can't leave him hanging. Everything he just admitted to me is exactly what I wanted to hear. It takes me a moment to gather the thoughts running amok through my head before I can respond.

"I didn't know exactly what I wanted to hear you say, but when you said it out loud. I realized it's exactly what I needed to hear you say. It gives me the courage to tell you that you're everything I've needed and wanted in a man. You've given me a sense of peace, comfort, and home that I haven't had in a relationship, and I don't want to let that go Collins. I know we said just the holidays, but I want more than that. More of us." I spit out, everything spills out easier than I thought it might.

Rather than responding, Collins gently nudges Precious off his lap, pulling me into the now vacant spot. My legs find their place on the outside of his thighs while his hands rest gently on my hips. I let mine wrap around his neck, resting my forehead on his.

"Am I dreaming, or did you just say that you want to be mine?" His lips tilt into a grin.

"You're not dreaming, and I do want to be yours." I laugh lightly.

"I'm going to kiss you now, okay?"

"Please do."

Collins moves one hand to the back of my head, pulling my lips to his. Our lips meet gently, but his cock jumps between my legs, causing me to gasp as it turns more heated.

"Can I take you to my room?" he asks between kisses.

"You better," I demand as he stands from the couch and walks us to his room.

Kicking the door open, Collins walks us to his bed,

making himself comfortable against the headboard as he continues kissing me, our need increasing the longer this goes on. I find myself grinding down into his lap while his hands roam over my body, ridding me of my clothes until the only thing between us is his sweats.

I reach for his waistband, but he traps my wrist, "One second."

He doesn't say anything, instead lifting me gently off his lap and positioning himself to lie flat on his back, "Now I'm ready."

"For what?" I ask in confusion.

"For you to sit that sweet cunt on my face. I've missed your taste."

"I... Uh, I don't know about that..."

"I'm not asking, Harls. Come over here and sit." He pauses, letting his hand run up and down my thigh, almost to the place I want him most, slowly causing a shiver to run through my body before adding, "Okay fine, please."

I lift myself to my knees and swing a leg over his head before gently hovering over his face.

"I said sit." Collins bands his arms around my thighs and pulls me down, my pussy connecting with his waiting tongue. He guides my movements over his face, devouring me. I'm helpless to do anything but moan and grab the headboard to keep from folding over. My hips grinding down onto his tongue as pleasure continues to wrack my body, but I need more. My hand moves to my breasts, rolling my nipples in time with my hips, and my head falling back in ecstasy.

When Collins removes one of his hands from my thigh

and groans begin to reverberate between my legs, I crane my neck around to see him stroking his cock, which causes a rush of wetness to leave my body.

"Fuck Collins, I'm getting close." My spine begins to stiffen, my thighs clasp around his head, and my heart races as I continue to ride his face.

When one long groan leaves Collins' throat, I let go, screaming his name, swiveling my hips until I'm fully sated before lifting myself and seeing Collins' face is completely soaked. Heat floods my cheeks, knowing that I caused this.

"Yep, definitely can't let you go now." He chuckles swiping his forearm across his lips before pulling my lips to his in a gentle kiss. "Let's get cleaned up."

After showering, Collins and I lay together talking, and by the time I fall asleep my cheeks hurt from smiling so much. I don't know how I got so lucky with him, but I'm not going to take it for granted.

"Let's get right into it, then shall we." Violet says as we settle into her office for our first session since she gave me the assignment of treating my time with Collins like it was real.

Over the next twenty minutes, I recount all of the events since New Years, leaving out the sexual parts because it's not necessary for her to know the nitty gritty details.

"It's a big step to be honest first and foremost to yourself, but also the people around you. So you should be proud of yourself for that." Violet ignores the rest of what I've said for now. We are, of course, here for me and while my relationship is important, my growth is the first thing we should talk about—I can appreciate that.

"I am. I thought it was going to be a lot harder than it was but when he all but handed me his truth over on a silver platter, I found it was much easier to do the same. I hesitated only for a moment because I truly wasn't expecting him to come home from his trip ready to do the same thing that I was."

"How are you feeling about moving forward with Collins?"

"I'm ready. I know that he won't hurt me, I know that he wants me just as much as I want to be with him, and I don't want to let us go. I have to admit there's still a lingering fear that maybe we won't work out or that Benji is going to show up and ruin everything—which is illogical because I haven't heard from him in months."

"Given all that you experienced with Benji, it's reasonable that you may be experiencing some fear, but you must continue to separate those two relationships and focus on the fact that, and correct me if I'm wrong here—Benji and Collins are two completely different people."

"That's one hundred percent correct, they are two different people. I know that I need to separate the two, and I *am* trying."

"Trying is just as important as doing. Plus, that's what I'm here for, to help navigate this among other things." She checks the small clock on her desk before adding, "Time's about up. Keep up the good work, and I'll see ya in a few weeks. Call me if anything changes."

"Thanks, Violet. See you!" I collect my belongings, and she walks me out of her office with a smile.

Chapter 19

Follow My Lead

Collins

I'm sitting on my back porch as the sun goes down, my finger hovering over the green call button of my phone screen. I take one final deep breath before letting my thumb press into my screen.

It rings and rings until a voice I've yearned to hear for years fills my phone, "Collins?"

"Hi, Mom." I respond, clearing my throat. Harley steps onto the porch, sitting beside me and letting her hand rest on my thigh. Silent support without being actively involved in the conversation.

"It's been a while. Is everything okay?" For the first time in a long time, I can hear concern for me from the person who should've been worried about me this whole time.

"Yes," I pause and Harley taps my thigh, encouraging me to tell the truth, "No acutally. I mean, physically I'm fine."

"Okay…"

"Mom, I called because I've missed you and Dad." I have to pause again, my eyes begin to water, "I know it's hard. I know that all you see when you look at me is Jordan, but I miss having parents. I miss you guys cheering me on at games. I miss spending the holidays with you both."

The line remains silent for a moment before a choked sob comes through the phone, and the fissure in my heart cracks open a little further.

"I-I'm sorry Mom. I didn't mean to make you upset." I add on through my own tears.

"Collins, my sweet boy. I feel terrible about the way that your father and I handled the passing of your brother. I regret every day not trying harder to make you feel seen and loved, for not reminding myself that I had two sons and one of them was feeling just as much, if not more, pain than we were. We miss you so much and we'd love a chance to get to know this version of you."

"It's okay, it wasn't easy for any of us, but I'd like that too. Would you guys want to come to a game, maybe?" Apprehension laces my tone because I don't know where they'd like to start, where we'd all be comfortable reacquainting ourselves with each other.

My mom clears her throat before speaking, "I think a hockey game may be too much, but if you're free in a few weeks, I'd love to cook for you."

"I understand, just know that invitation always stands."

"I'll remember that. We'll see you in a few weeks, okay. We love you."

"Love you too." I hang up the phone and heave a deep

breath out, trying to process every emotion and words that were traded between my mom and I.

"You handled that really well, from the parts I heard at least." Harley mentions from beside me.

"Thank you. That was tough, but I'm glad that I did it."

"Me too."

"You'll come to dinner with me?" I question, hoping the answer isn't no, because I don't know if I can handle this without her.

"Absolutely."

It's family skate night. Honestly, one of my favorite nights of the year, I have my friends, the kids, and Harley but I can't help but feel like people are missing. Jordan and I would've been racing back and forth across the rink much like Dom and Conrad do now. My parents would've been cuddled up by the hot cocoa stand watching us act like fools, but I gave up inviting them to stuff like this a long time ago.

"Hey, can you help me tie these up?" Harley asks where she's sitting down in front of me. My Manta Rays hoodie covers her and dark skinny jeans mold to her thighs perfectly. A picture of perfection with two loose braids and light makeup sitting on her face. *All mine.*

"Always." I drop to one knee in front of her, lifting her foot over my leg so that I can lace her up properly. I work quickly, ready to get her out onto the ice with me. When

Kodi and Mav showed up to the first family skate night two years ago, I couldn't help but stare at her as she and Sin attempted to skate around the rink, being too stubborn to ask for help.

"You feel like your skating skills have improved at all?" I ask, helping her stand, she wobbles for a moment before righting herself.

"Definitely, I've been to three of these now and I have a pro to help keep me balanced." A cheeky grin spreads across her face as she begins to walk toward the ice.

"Oh my God! Look at Bella go!" she squeals excitedly, pointing to where Mav and Bella skate side by side. Bella's cheeks puff out air as she pushes her little legs to keep herself moving.

"She's doing so well! I can't believe she's already moving so easily on her own." I respond happily.

"Go, Bella, go!" Kodi claps excitedly as she watches them skate. Bella turns her head to her Mama, which causes her to lose her balance, but Mav's there to catch her before she hits the ground, and they're off to the races again.

"Alright, let's skate Peppermint." I step out onto the ice first, with Harley following, her hand in mine.

I move a little faster than Harley at first before she huffs, "Some of us don't skate five days a week. Slow down!"

"Sorry." I slow my pace to match hers, forgetting that for some people skating isn't like walking and that I'm not in a conditioning or a game. I'm enjoying a casual skate with my friends, my girl, and my teammates.

We skate a few laps as Harley finds her footing before I turn on my heel, skating backward so I can watch her move toward me. A light smile graces her face, the occasional laugh slipping out as she loosens up, enjoying herself more and more with each lap.

Eventually, Tate rolls up beside me, Hayden in his arms, "take him for a few laps so I can skate with Darcy?

"You got it. Hey, Hayden! Want to go so fast?" I ask my nephew, who claps his chubby hands, a small, toothy smile across his reddened cheeks.

"I'm going to tap out, but I can take him when you're done, so that Dom can and I quote 'run circles around you before the night ends.' Plus, the girls and I have to have a gossip session." Harley smiles at me as she steps out of the rink. I give her a salute as she waves us off.

Hayden and I skate two laps before I hand him off to Harley.

"Montez!" I holler across the rink, Dom turns toward my voice, a shit eating grin on his face.

"Ready for our annual family skate night race?" He waggles his eyebrows at me as he approaches.

"You're going down."

"You wish."

"Alright, fellas. You know the rules. Three laps. No shoving, pushing, tripping. First one back to me gets bragging rights and loser buys everybody hot chocolate." Nik announces formally as Dom and I take our spots on either side of him. Mav stands on the other side of the rink at the same position as Nik.

Nik begins his countdown, and then we are off to the races.

"Don't be a sore loser, babe." Harley teases from my side as we follow everyone out of the arena. Dom destroyed me out there, but I was a little distracted by an idea that hit me as I watched Harley cheer me on from outside the glass.

"I'm not a sore loser."

"Anything I can do to help cheer you up?" She pinches my arm.

"Actually... There is. Follow my lead." I whisper for only her, a mischievous grin spreading across her face.

"Damn it! I left my wallet back there." I curse aloud, patting my pockets dramatically as our friends all turn toward us. "You all go ahead, we'll see you at Hayden's party next weekend."

Everyone says their goodbyes, although Nik chuckles in my ears, "Have fun, dude."

I turn on my heel, Harley following closely behind me. Rather than taking her back into the arena, I take a sharp left, guiding her up to the box that Maverick typically rents out for our big games.

"Where are you taking me?" She whisper-shouts at me, "are we even supposed to be here?"

"Nope, and you'll see." I continue up the stairs and push open the door to the box before pulling her inside and locking the door behind us, trapping her between myself and the door. Leaning down, I nip gently at her neck.

"You're right, I am a sore loser, and I wanted to show

you something." I breathe into her neck before turning and guiding her over to the front row of seats.

"Do you recognize this view?" I ask, pushing my hips forward into hers, pressing them into the railing.

"I do. We sit here for games."

"Did you know that if I squint hard enough, I can see you watching me?" I let my hand move to the front of her pants, toying with the button.

"No." She breathes.

"So I thought, I'd come up here and see what the view is like." I pop the button on her jeans, yanking them down quickly before pushing her upper half forward so she's forced to lean on the railing, jutting her ass toward me.

"We're going to have to be quick, and I need you to be quiet for me. Can you do that, Baby?" I ask, unbuckling and pushing down my own jeans then stroking my cock lightly.

"Yes." She whispers, swaying her hips slightly.

Reaching between us, I let two fingers find her entrance, pushing in and out to find her soaking wet already.

"What's got you so worked up, Harley?" I continue to toy with her and myself.

"Fuck, Collins. Watching you on the ice, knowing you could see me watching, you holding a baby, just you in general." She keens softly.

I remove my fingers, placing one hand on her hip and gently pushing her legs further apart. Reaching into my wallet, I quickly slide on a condom before notching my cock at her entrance and filling her in one thrust. Her gasp fills the space around us, echoing slightly.

"Quiet, Baby. You don't want us to get caught, do you?" I gently move my free hand to cover her mouth as I continue to thrust in and out of her. She bites my palm, causing me to remove my hand, "Feisty."

A giggle leaves her mouth that quickly turns into a gasp when that hand begins rubbing tight circles around her clit. Her moans begin to crescendo, her body meeting mine with every thrust–until she suddenly goes still.

"What happened?" I ask, concerned.

"There's someone down there," she whispers, looking toward the rink where the zamboni runs over the ice.

"It's okay. He wears headphones and never looks up." I slowly begin moving again.

When she doesn't push back, I reel her back into focusing on me. My hands toying with her clit and nipples, her body slowly beginning to relax for me, "Just focus on me, Baby. I can feel how close you are."

"Your body was made for me." I continue to encourage as those telltale tingles begin at the base of my spine, and her pussy begins to tighten.

"Give it to me, Harls." Her body seizes and she begins to scream my name, but I quiet her again with my palm, taking me over the edge with her.

She whimpers as I pull myself from her, heading to the bar to grab some napkins to clean us up.

"That was fun," she says as we redress.

"It was, we could do it again sometime."

"Sounds like you want to get caught." She smirks as I unlock the door and guide her toward the parking garage to my Tacoma.

"Not that I *want* to get caught, but it's the thrill of potentially getting caught."

"Like New Years?"

"Yes, like New Years." I open the door of the truck, helping her inside and buckling her seatbelt.

"I can do that myself, you know?" she goads.

"I know, but I like to do it for you." I peck her lips before taking my seat behind the wheel and driving us back to my place.

Chapter 20

One Happy Dude

Harley

Missing Darcy's baby shower is one of the biggest regrets I have from the fallout that was my relationship with Benji. Now sitting here with my best friends as we tie up party favors, setting up food and decor for Hayden's first birthday party, I feel that regret slowly lifting off my shoulders. I'm here now, and I've got a man who encourages me to spend time with my friends.

Darcy and Rose–Tatum's mom have brought the theme "One Happy Dude" to life with the smiley face, checkerboards mixed with yellows envelop the beach house. The guys took Hayden and Bella out for lunch so we could focus on getting everything set up.

"Everything looks so good!" Kodi claps as she rounds the kitchen hallway, a stack of presents wrapped haphazardly in her arms.

"Who... Wrapped those?" Sin asks, her nose scrunched in distaste.

"My son's father did his best, okay? He asked me not to help." Darcy volleys back. I know it's driving her nuts that she couldn't go back and rewrap the gifts.

"Alrighty then." I choke on a laugh.

"An hour until party time and everything except the foods that need to stay chilled are set out, wine and girl talk on the deck?" Enid suggests, from the other side of the room, where she just finished setting up the photo area.

"Yes, please. Red or white?" Darcy asks as she pulls both bottles from the fridge. Red is almost a unanimous decision, aside from Kodi, who stays suspiciously quiet as we walk out to the deck, all taking our seats on the wooden furniture.

Darcy passes glasses to each of us, then pours a hefty amount of wine into each of our tumblers.

"Trying to get us drunk before your child's party?" Sin teases.

"Eh, just something to take the edge off before I have to *people*." Darcy shrugs, and we all chuckle at her response.

After twenty or so minutes, we've all finished our glasses, but Kodi's is still full to the brim.

I elbow her while the other girls are talking about how Mace has his first crush and Enid doesn't know how to handle all the testosterone she's surrounded by.

"Babes, you better admit why you're not drinking or pour that into mine before someone says something," I whisper to her, there's only one reason she wouldn't be indulging, and although she hasn't said it, my intuition knows.

"I don't want to take away from Hayden, D, and Tate's day." The exasperation is heavy in her tone.

"Do you think that your best friend in the entire world is going to be mad at you for your dream of finally becoming a mom coming true?" I encourage.

"No, obviously not."

"So then spit it out."

Kodi coughs, setting her wine glass down and grabbing the other's attention. "I have some news."

We all sit quietly in anticipation, wondering what she's doing to say, but I can see all of the hope glimmering behind our eyes.

"I'm pregnant!" Her voice filled with emotion–excitement, fear, anticipation. A cacophony of squeals breaks loose as we all stand, surrounding her, saying our congratulations, and peppering her with questions regarding our future niece or nephew.

The noise draws Rose's attention from where she sits on the couch, scrolling through her phone. She stands and joins us on the deck, where another chorus of noise ensues as we all share the excitement of Kodi and Maverick's pregnancy.

"Okay, so to answer questions. I found out right after Christmas, we don't know the gender, everything looks good, morning sickness does last all day just like D told me and yes you all will obviously be planning my baby shower." Kodi says after we've calmed down.

"This is so exciting! Do you have baby shower themes chosen already?" Darcy asks.

"Duh. For a girl, I'm thinking 'A Little Cutie is on the Way' and for a boy 'Slice, Slice, Baby' because that's all I've been craving." Kodi responds enthusiastically.

"Um, love those." I say.

"Oooooo if we do pizza, we can order New York style from that one place downtown that's so freaking good and serves the slices as big as your head." Enid cheers.

"Well, I know what I'm making Mav pick up for dinner tonight." Kodi laughs.

"Same." We all decide together.

As soon as Maverick and Bella arrive for Hayden's party, we once again broke out in congratulations.

Strong arms wrap around me from behind as I stand with Enid and Conrad, as party guests continue to flow into the beach house.

"Hi, Peppermint." Collins' silky voice fills my ears, I turn giving him my attention.

"Hey there." I smile at him, taking in the loose curl that dangles over his forehead, the plain navy t-shirt that's sculpted to his chest, and the chinos that hang from his hips.

"You look very pretty today."

"Thank you. So do you."

Collins laughs before pulling me in for a quick kiss, then turning me back toward Enid and Conrad, keeping his arms linked around me.

"How is everything going for y'all?" Conrad prods.

"Pretty good, just taking it day by day. Enjoying our

time together." Collins responds easily, like he didn't even have to think about what he was going to say.

Enid smiles loopily, "I'm obsessed with you guys."

"I feel like every time I leave her with you girls, she gets wine drunk." Conrads accuses.

"Blame Darcy, she wanted to be buzzed before she had to host." I shrug, "Plus Enid is fine. She's got you to make sure she gets home okay."

Conrad blushes away from my comment, I think he's still having a hard time accepting that Enid and Mace's life is better with him in it.

The next hours fly by as we watch Hayden open gifts, run around with the other kids, and enjoy food. At some point, Tatum scoops Hayden up from the living room, rushing to his nursery after making a quick stop by Darcy. She moves around the kitchen, getting an area ready for his smash cake, looking back toward the nursery every once in a while.

"If everyone wants to gather around the island, we're going to do Hayden's cake once Tatum gets him changed." Darcy's voice carries through the area, and we all move together to join her near the kitchen.

Kodi walks toward Darcy, keeping her facing away from the hallway, which is weird because I imagine she'd want to see her son come out for his first cake smash. That is until Tatum steps out of the hallway, setting Hayden on the ground as he whispers something to his son before sending him toward Darcy. I grab Collins' hand and Sin's, squeezing the life out of them as the realization of what's happening falls over the room.

Hayden pulls on the end of Darcy's dress, and she

turns, picking him up off the ground, "Hey bud, I thought you were supposed t—" and sees Tatum on one knee behind her.

Tatum proposes, and we try to keep our excitement hushed, although I'm sure they hear us shout "Oh my God!" and by the end, we are all in tears. Turns out the guys and Kodi knew what was happening, but the rest of us were left in the dark so that Darcy's surprise wouldn't be ruined.

I'm once again reminded that I may have missed out on two of my best friends' big news today if I hadn't walked away from Benji all those months ago.

Chapter 21

Natural Feeling

Collins

As we park in front of my childhood home, every emotion under the sun is pulsing beneath my veins. My hand taps away on the steering wheel as I ponder if we should just turn around and drive back to my place.

Warmth envelops my hand, and Harley draws my attention away from the thoughts, "It'll be okay. They're excited to see you, it might be awkward at first, but I think that's to be expected. Plus, I'll be here, ready to support you in whatever way you need."

"Okay, it's weird being back here after all this time."

"That's a natural feeling too. Hopefully, it can feel like home again for you soon."

"I already have a home and it's with you," I tell her, a pink hue paints the apples of her cheeks, and she gives me that shy smile I love so much.

"Maybe this can feel like a happy place again. Better?"

"I'll take it. Let's go, I think I've stalled enough." I hop out of the truck and jog around to help Harley out. Immediately taking her hand, to keep me grounded as we approach the brick home with a bright blue front door that mom insisted was a stylistic choice.

I knock twice, and the door swings open almost immediately. We're greeted by my parents and the smells of what I think is homemade spaghetti—something my mom cooked often when we were growing up, even shredding a block of parmesan herself.

Mom's lip begins to quiver immediately, and my dads grip around her arm tightens in support.

"Hi." I try to smile at them, but my head feels foggy, I know I'm here with them but it doesn't feel real.

"Hi! You made it." While her lip still quivers, my mom smiles back at me. She opens her arms to me, and I don't know if I can handle her arms around me but I don't want to deny her this moment. Harley gently squeezes my hand, encouraging me before letting it go so I can step forward into my mom's embrace.

"Hello, Mr. McKee. I'm Harley." Harley introduces herself to my dad while my mom clutches me closely like I may slip through her fingers, like my brother did all those years ago.

"Francis, honey I think you might be suffocating him," my dad teases.

"Oh, right, sorry." She steps back wiping her hands down her apron, "supper is just about ready if you all want to have a seat at the dining table."

"Do you need any help?" Harley offers.

"No, sweetie but thank you." Mom responds with a tenderness in her voice, like she can already tell the type of person Harley is and that she's perfect for me. How can she know that when she doesn't even know me anymore? I'm not quite sure, maybe mother"s intuition.

Mom turns on her heel, heading to the kitchen and my father follows closely behind her, I assume, ensuring she's okay and giving me a moment to process as well. I grasp Harley's hand again, guiding her further into the house and observing all of the details. Honestly, it seems as if nothing's changed, pictures line the walls, it smells the same—clean like lemons, and the only change I've noticed is they've gotten a new couch.

"It's basically the same," I observe.

"A home well-loved and lived in doesn't need constant changing," Harley responds. I think her underlying message is that when people go through a traumatic experience, they hang on to every thread of that old life. The life where that person was still around, or when they hadn't gone through that experience.

We continue further into the home, veering right into the dining room, where I pull out Harley's seat, taking the one beside her.

"Do you two drink sweet tea?" My dad asks, poking his head out of the kitchen entryway.

"Yep," I say while Harley confirms with a nod.

"You doing okay?" she asks quietly.

"Oddly enough, I feel comfortable. There isn't the tension like I expected. Sadness sure but that I knew would linger being here again."

"Good." She pecks me on the cheek before my parents join us. Carrying spaghetti, garlic bread, a salad, and drinks for us.

"Thank you, everything looks delicious," Harley expresses.

"I hope it tastes as good as it looks." My mom chuckles.

"If it's anything like when I was younger, I'm sure its going to be wonderful," I add in.

We pass platters around, eating quietly for a bit before my dad speaks up, "Son, how's the season going?"

"Don't play coy, Ken, you know how the season's going and don't even try to hide the fact that you have his jersey in your closet." Mom calls my dad out, and he chokes on a piece of garlic bread.

"You do?" I ask, my head spinning because all this time I thought they hadn't been paying attention to my career.

Once Dad's got his bearings back, he speaks, "Um... Yeah we've watched every game you've played. Seems like you guys are on track for a cup win and Hoyer seems to be doing very well fitting in as well."

"Yeah, we've all been working our asses off to get into the finals again. I think we've got it in the bag this year." My voice filling the area with palpable excitement over the fact that we might get our second cup win in two years and over the fact that my parents have been supporting my team silently for years.

"They've been incredible on the ice. You both should join me for a game one night." Harley recommends, she knows I'd love to have all three of them in the stands cheering me on.

"We'll have to arrange that. What is it that you do for work, Harley?" Mom questions.

"Oh, I'm a licensed mental health counselor. I work at the Right Place, Right Time center with troubled youth and kids."

"That must be a difficult job," Dad comments.

"It's got its ups and downs but I wouldn't trade it for the world. I've known for a very long time that I wanted to help people; I just hadn't pinpointed what community. I interned with them in my undergrad, and it solidified that was the community I wanted to work with. Then they offered me a job with flexibility while I finished school and I haven't looked back." The passion that Harley carries into her career can be heard in every word she speaks.

"Sounds like you've got a good one." My mom sounds thrilled.

"I intend to keep her forever if she'll have me." I smile at my mom, then at my girl.

Her cheeks taking on that pink blush again, "I think I like the sound of that."

After finishing dinner, we move to the living room, chatting about life and recalling memories we had as a family before Mom forces freshly baked chocolate chip cookies onto us. When the sun starts to set, we decide it's time to head out.

"Thank you for tonight. I hope we can do it again." Harley thanks my parents as she steps away from a hug.

"Please! You are both welcome anytime." My mom states happily.

"Thanks again," I say, hugging my mom and then my dad.

"I'm proud of you, son. Thank you for giving us another chance," My dad says just for me, and it causes my eyes to well with tears once again.

"See you guys later."

Chapter 22

Love of my Life

Harley

hat a long day. I had clients back to back, a meeting with my boss, and cannot wait to spend my evening with Collins. I'm not sure what he has planned for us, but time with him is just the reprieve I need to reset before another day of work tomorrow.

Stepping out into the humid, Florida air, I see Collins waiting patiently in his Tacoma to my right, a smile pasted on his face. Then I notice the car that I've only seen in the occasional nightmare since a little over a year ago. The beat up, brown, twenty-year-old Miata sits across the parking lot —its engine humming lowly. I can feel my shoulders scrunch up, my stomach roiling uncomfortably, and my heart starts pounding away in my chest as Benji throws the door open and paces toward me.

I notice that rage isn't painting his features, but his bright red face is covered in wetness which tells me all I need to know. He's here to gaslight me, attempt to win me back, but I don't need him anymore. I don't want to hear his words, but if I don't I'm scared what might happen. I freeze, unable to move as I wait to see what's coming for me. I glance in Collins' direction noticing he's ready to jump in, but a quick head shake tells him to stay put... For now.

Benji stops about a foot in front of me, crocodile tears rolling down his face as he waits for any sort of reaction from me.

"What are you doing here?" Clearing my throat as I speak, it's all I can manage for now.

"I missed my girl. I noticed your car wasn't here, so I was hoping that I could pick you up, take you out. I need to have you back in my life. I've been miserable without you. My sunshine on a rainy day," he says with an attempt at a weak smile. He must not have noticed Collins yet; that's probably a good thing.

"Benji, I don't think that's a good idea. I'm not interested, and I think I made that very clear to you when I walked away. Also, by the ignored texts and phone calls."

"I thought you just needed a break, Baby. I've changed, I promise. I just want the best for you. I can be that, you remember how good I was to you, right?" His voice tenses the slightest bit before returning to an even tone.

Yep, being neglectful, accusing me of cheating, not letting me leave your apartment, and leaving bruises. *So so good to me.*

"It wasn't a break, Benji, it's been almost a year. I've healed and I won't put myself back into this cycle with you."

In a move I'm not expecting, he drops to a knee pulling

out a small velvet box. I gasp because what the fuck does he think he's doing right now?

"Get up," I demand because I'm not putting up with this behavior, we aren't getting married and he's fully delusional if he thinks we are, and I refuse to get pulled back into his cycle.

He seems shocked before letting his head hang low as he wails. Expecting comfort, maybe? He won't be getting that from me, along with anything else he thinks is going to happen by him blindsiding me at my job.

"Now, Benji!" I command again because his tears mean nothing to me.

His head whips up, and I see the shift. The way that his "pain" morphs into rage, his eyes darken, and his fists ball at his sides before he's back on his feet. I give Collins another quick nod to wait it out, but this time Benji notices.

"What the fuck is he doing here?" He bellows, stepping closer but still not in my face.

"Picking me up from work, my car was in the shop," I say casually, although the perspiration forming on my forehead and the back of my neck would give away my nervousness.

"You're not leaving with him," Benji orders.

"That's not your choice to make." I take one step back, and Benji takes one forward.

"You'll regret it if you do." His threat is one that would normally have me cowering, but I find myself squaring my shoulders, standing my ground.

"You don't get to tell me what to do anymore, Benji."

"Oh, Sunshine, that wasn't me telling you what to do.

That was just a simple statement about how we're going to move forward now."

"There is no *we*, hasn't been in a long time. You know that." I tell him softly.

"There is a *we*, always has been. You just forgot because you needed to see he wasn't it for you, that I was." His smile is menacing as he speaks.

I just stare at him, I have nothing left to say, and my silence may set him off but I'm ready for this conversation to be over. Just as I thought, he begins to rampage.

"You're a fucking whore!" His voice booms in my face, and he steps closer to me, almost in my face. "You told me you didn't have feelings for him! You said over and over again there was nothing to worry about, and now what? You're sleeping in his bed, riding his cock, letting him touch you?"

"It's none of your business, and I think it's time for you to leave." I try to step away but he steps forward again, hand grasping my forearm in a way that I know is going to bruise once he lets go.

"I told you that you aren't leaving with him. Just because you ran to him and let him think he had a chance while you waited for me to come back. He means nothing to you, I know that." He begins to pull me toward his car, and the adrenaline that I've felt since he showed up is beginning to wear off. I can't pull back, but I don't have to because the next thing I know Benji's hands are no longer on me, and I'm wrapped in the warmth of Collins' vanilla and spice smell, instantly relaxing into his touch.

"Don't get up. I will not hesitate to lay your ass out on the concrete again. The police are already on their way, so don't bother trying to leave. You'll only make it worse." Collins commands Benji, who only gives him a whimper in return from where he's nursing one eye.

Collins turns his attention to me next, "Are you hurt?"

"No."

"You're sure?"

I nod in response, still trying to bring myself back into this moment.

"Do you want to wait in the truck?" I nod again before he guides me over and helps me slide into the passenger seat, where we sit and wait for the authorities to arrive.

When they do, they speak to Collins first before letting Benji say his side. I don't hear any of it, but I do hear him whining about a lawyer as they throw him into the back seat of a cruiser. When it's my turn, I give my statement, say yes to going down to the station to file a restraining order, and tell them I have no idea if he's been showing up here for months or just today because I don't. I've not noticed him, haven't received a phone call or text in months, and thought I was out of his grip.

This time, though, I am free. If he does try again, there are protections in place for me. There should've been a long time ago, like the officer said, but I could never bring myself to face him that way again until I wasn't given a choice.

If you were to ask me how I ended up in bed with Collins wrapped around me, Precious mewling into my neck, I wouldn't be able to tell you. This is how I know that Collins is exactly who I need and want to spend my life with.

"Are you sure you're okay? You've been pretty quiet." He murmurs into my hair while his free hands stroke my back.

"I think this evening was just a lot. But I don't know what I would have done without you being there for me. Without you getting me home, without your arms to keep me safe." I whisper into the quiet of his bedroom.

"I wouldn't want to be anywhere else tonight. Even if it wasn't what we had in mind, there's always tomorrow."

"Do you want that?"

"Do I want that?" He pauses as if the question bewilders him. "Of course I fucking do. I want every night, every kiss, every tear for as long as you'll let me have them Harley."

"You do?" Now I'm the one who is confused.

"That's what I said, isn't it, Peppermint?" Now he's pulled my attention to his eyes, forcing me to stay with him, not letting me shy away from letting him see the emotion swimming in his blue orbs.

"It is what you said."

"Have I ever told you anything I didn't mean?"

"No." I try to bite back the smile threatening to escape.

"And I never will because you, Harley Wheeler, are *the* love of my life." He doesn't let me respond, pulling me in for a gentle kiss, solidifying us.

When we pull apart, I'm able to tell him, "and you, Collins McKee, are mine."

Chapter 23

In Private

Collins ‖ 10 months later

After last year's Christmas trip, our little family has decided to make this an annual thing. We continue to expand with Kodi and Maverick adding Aurora to their family just under two months ago. Very brave of them to drive multiple states with a newborn and a five year old but I know they loved every second of it. While Harley and I aren't adding children anytime soon, I will officially be making her mine forever come Christmas morning and proposing here, where our journey started. Where it was all supposed to be fake and end after the holidays but here I am lying in bed with Harley, my wildest dream of her telling me she wanted to be mine, having come true just ten months ago.

What she doesn't know is that my parents are coming up on Christmas Eve and will be present for our engagement. I'm grateful for the opportunity to have them involved in our lives going forward. We've taken the time to reacquaint ourselves with each other, to bond and rebuild the relationship we once had. It's not perfect, and there are times when I can tell that they wish Jordan were here however, I feel that too. I don't feel neglected or ignored like I did as a teen. I wonder how different our holidays would look, how excited Jordan would've been to help me design Harley's engagement ring, or one day being the uncle that chases his nieces or nephews around the ice.

"Are you excited for tomorrow?" I ask her as we settle into bed on Christmas Eve.

"Very, last year was a core memory and I'm ready to make more with everyone."

"Me too." The elation over my plans for tomorrow laced beneath my tone.

"You seem a little too excited." The slightest bit of suspicion comes through as she speaks, so I try to stay cool as our conversation continues.

"Just ready to spend the morning with everyone, eat whatever Nik is cooking up, and see what gifts everyone gives. I feel like everyone's love language is gift giving."

"I'm inclined to agree, Freckles. I have your gift ready, and I'm so excited to share it with you."

"You sure you don't want to give it to me now?" I tease, knowing that she absolutely will not. She'll want to see mine and everyone else's reaction when I open it.

"Nope." She pops the p. "You won't be getting it until tomorrow night..."

"Tomorrow night?" I find myself boxing her into the bed with my body, now *very* curious as to what it is.

"Mhmmm in private." A sensual grin painting her full lips.

"Well in that case, I can't wait." I wiggle my eyebrows at her before planting a kiss on her lips, settling behind her and pulling her back into my arms, "Better get some sleep then. Goodnight, I love you."

"Goodnight, Collins. I love you." She chuckles at me as we resettle back into bed, watching a light snow fall outside the cabin's window.

"Merry Christmas!" A chorus of voices greets us as we step into the main cabin. The smells of Christmas fill the space—cinnamon, spices, peppermint, and maple syrup. Nik has his back turned to us, working away on something that looks like cinnamon rolls by the stove, Kodi feeds Rory on the couch while Hayden and Bella play with a train set on the living room floor, and Darcy appears to be piecing together a charcuterie board at the table. Looking around the area, I don't see my parents, but I confirmed with Mav via text that they're up in their room and will join us for breakfast shortly.

"Merry Christmas!" We shout back in unison.

Then my Mom's voice fills the air, "Merry Christmas, honey."

Harley turns toward the steps leading up to the second level of the cabin—confusion then awe passes over her features.

"What are your parents doing here? Why didn't you tell

me?" she asks me before hurrying toward my parents to wrap them in a hug.

"We just didn't want to miss Christmas with you all. We made it in late last night and didn't want to wake you." My dad affirms, winking at me over his shoulder.

"I'm glad you're here." I smile, approaching to embrace my parents once they've released Harley.

We spend the next twenty minutes talking to my parents about their drive before Nik bellows, "Breakfast is ready, let's eat!"

After we've all eaten our weight in breakfast foods and accoutrements, we gather around the tree to open gifts. The ring sits heavily in my flannel pajama pant pocket that matches Harley's nightgown. I try not to fiddle with it too much to avoid drawing Harley's attention. Everyone laughs, smiles, and even a few tears are shed as gifts are passed around the room.

Once all of the wrapping paper and boxes are thrown out, we get ready for photos. Harley and I stand in front of the tree smiling toward Sin's camera for a moment before I drop to one knee and the room erupts in gasps. Harley glitches for a moment when she sees me beside her with the dark green velvet box opened up—looking at me then Sin in shock and back to me honing in on the ring and my shaky hands. Her head begins to nod before I even have the chance to pop the question, and I hear my mom chuckle through her sniffles as she watches on.

"Peppermint?" I choke on her nickname.

"Collins?" Tears already welling in her eyes.

"Getting to know and love you over the past year has been all the time I need to know that I don't want to spend my life with anyone else. No one else to share my heart, my tears, my life, or my home with. Would you do me the honor of marrying me?"

She surprises me when instead of saying yes, she says, "I would rather share one lifetime with you than face all the ages of this world alone."

"I thought I had wandered into a dream." I pause, adding, "That's a yes for those of you who are not nerds."

The room erupts in cheers, I'm sure the rest of our friend group has no idea that we were referencing an epic love declaration, but it doesn't matter—in this moment, all I see is Harley looking down at me as I slide the intricate ring onto her finger. The seminavette-shaped diamond has moss running through it, the band an intricate intertwining of vines. Harley pulls me up from my kneeling position, crashing her lips into mine before pulling back and letting everyone else celebrate with us.

After more pictures, and spending time with our family, we're now back in the A-frame. Harley stepped into the bathroom to clean up and get my gift ready, so I've busied myself with tidying up downstairs.

"Collins," Harley purrs from the top of the staircase. My eyes may have popped out of my head, and my cock hardens immediately when I lay eyes on the vision that is my future wife. Her curls sit around her face, wearing a bright red lipstick, but the star of the show is the red, satin body suit fit to her curves. If I pulled the bow sitting on her chest, her entire body would be exposed to me and I intend to do just that.

Running up the stairs, she steps backward toward the

bed, taking a seat and spreading her legs wide, welcoming me to the space.

"This is my Christmas present?" I ask, pulling gently on the bow so as not to unravel her outfit quite yet.

"Mhmmm," she says breathlessly.

"And I get to unwrap you?"

"You can do whatever you want."

"Oh, I have so many plans for you tonight, *fiancé*." That's when I tug on the bow, releasing her breasts for me.

"Up, Peppermint. I want to see the rest of you." She stands quickly, and I pull the rest of the lingerie off. Looking to the corner where a small tree sits, an idea comes to me.

"You up to trying something new for me tonight?" I ask, holding her chin up to me.

"Always."

"That's my girl. Lie back for me." I head toward the small tree, unraveling the lights and coming back to her.

"What're you going to do with those?" She questions, not concerned, but curious. I've tied her up a few times as we've explored our sexual interests together, but never like this.

Rather than answering, I get to work. Plugging the lights in beside the bed, I make quick work of tying Harley's wrists together, wrapping them around her chest and rendering her unable to move her upper half.

"Everything feel okay?" I want to make sure she's comfortable and give her the option to stop.

"Better than." I catch her rubbing her thighs together in anticipation of what's to come.

"Good, I've been waiting to see you like this since last December." I let my eyes roam over her, the way her chest is pushed out, the slight tension from the lights causing her nipples to pucker, and the wetness gathering between her thighs.

"Where should I start?" I ponder aloud as I undress before placing myself between her thighs again.

"Here?" I let my thumb smear her red lipstick across her cheek, she sucks it into her mouth for a moment, causing my dick to twitch against her.

"Or here?" I leave a smattering of kisses along her face, neck, and chest before pulling a taut nipple into my mouth. Sucking and pulling as she moans beneath me, I know she'd love to run her fingers through my hair, but making her desperate and needy so that when I sink inside her she's ready for me is my priority.

"Or maybe here?" I ask, moving even lower on her body, gently blowing air on her wet pussy, which causes her to squirm beneath me.

"There, please, Collins, there." She begs.

"Already so needy for me, Baby?" I toy with her, leaving barely there touches along her pussy.

"Since you put this ring on my finger. All I've been able to think about is riding your cock."

"We'll get there. Right now I'm going to make you cum for me... a few times." I let my fingers spread her cunt before running my tongue up her slit and circling her clit. Her hips jerk up to my mouth, seeking the friction she needs to get there. I spread her legs wider, holding her down so she stays right where I want her.

Whimpers fill the air as she gets frustrated with me keeping her on the edge. Her hips continue to cant toward my tongue as I enjoy the taste of her.

"Collins, please."

"Please, what?"

"Let me cum. I need it." She whines. I let her legs free, inserting a finger into her cunt she pulls me in and I ease another in while my tongue continues to ravage her clit. Her moans crescendo into a scream as her orgasm takes over. I let her ride it out, and when she relaxes into the bed, I gently unwrap her from the lights, massaging her wrists before flipping us so she's on top of me.

"I think I remember you telling me you wanted to ride my cock?" I tease.

"I did." She grinds over my dick, rubbing her wetness over me.

Pulling her down to me, I grip the back of her neck, pulling her in for a rough kiss, "Do it for me then."

She moans into my mouth as our tongues tangle together, and she continues to rub herself over me. When we separate, she lifts herself off of me, positioning my cock at her entrance and sliding down slowly, causing me to groan as she buries me in her pussy.

She sits for a moment, not moving, looking down into my eyes as she plucks at her nipples. It's driving me crazy, I'm teetering on the edge of taking over, and I want her to move so badly but I can't blame her for playing games with me after I tied her up and teased her.

"Harley, Baby, I need you to move." I growl out my comment just as my cock twitches inside her, causing her to swivel her hips.

My hands grip her ass tightly as she lifts herself off me, her pussy is choking my cock as she continues to bounce up and down. Her speed increases, and I know my piercing has hit its mark when she begins to spasm around me, a sob of pleasure escapeing her throat. It takes me right over the edge with her.

Once we've cleaned up, we watch snow fall out the window, Precious curled at the edge of the bed as Harley tells me about her dream wedding. I fully intend to make her every wish come true, not just now but for the rest of our lives together.

Epilogue ‖ Best Honeymoon Ever

Collins ‖ One year later

Standing at the head of the aisle with my best friends standing beside me, I anxiously await Harley to appear as soft music begins to play. When she turns the corner, coming into view, my heart implodes, I choke on a sob, letting out the breath I've been holding. My almost wife approaches in a corset dress covered in flower appliques, she opted for a cape-style veil rather than the traditional type. A small bouquet of wildflowers in her hands that she passes off to Sin when she reaches the altar.

"Take a breath," Sin reminds Harley as she fixes her dress behind her. I give Harley an affirming nod and watch her blow out a slow breath that only I can see.

"Dude, she's gorgeous," Dom whispers from behind me, and I'm not sure if he's talking about Sin or my fiancé. The girls stand behind Harley in velvet, emerald green dresses, tissues tucked into their bouquets—I wish I had stuck some in my suit pocket.

"Baby, you look beautiful." I can't help but let my tears fall as I continue to take her in, noticing the Lothlorien leaf jewels adorning her hair that match my cufflinks.

"Thank you, we're getting married!" She squeaks just enough for me.

"We are right now." I wink at her, and our officiant begins the ceremony.

"We are gathered here today to witness the joining of..." His voice fades out because no one else exists to me during our wedding ceremony, all I see is my Peppermint, all I hear is her voice (and the officiants), and all I'm thinking about is kissing my bride.

Our exchange of vows is quick and easy, we've written private ones that we plan to share just between us when we arrive at our honeymoon destination—neither of us wanting more attention than necessary today. We've always been private in that way, our intimacy staying between us (mostly) and our confessions happening in the dark, wrapped in each other's arms.

Harley squeezes my hand as we slide rings onto their prospective fingers, and when the officiant states that I may now kiss my bride, I pull her into me. A small gasp leaving her mouth before my lips crash to hers, dipping her backward for the perfect photo, then standing her upright.

"I'd like to introduce you all to Mr. and Mrs. Collins McKee!" Our officiant states, the area fills with claps as Harley and I make our way to the bridal suite, the bridal party to the groomsmen room, while the rest of our guests get moved to the reception site for cocktail hour.

When the door shuts behind us, silence enveloping us, I find myself staring at *my wife*. The sense of protection I've felt over her increases tenfold, the fire burning in my heart for her suddenly blazing like Dante's inferno, and my cock threatens to burst out of its zipper.

"Why are you looking at me like that?" The shy Harley, the one who loves when I look at her like this, but also squirms under the heat of my stares comes to the forefront—eyes wide and puffy lips pursed.

"Just thinking. Come here." I open my arms, pulling her into me gently without ruining her hair or makeup... until tonight at least.

"Thinking about?"

"How we went from fake boyfriend and girlfriend to married. How lucky I am to call you mine until I take my last breath. How fucking in love I am with you and have been since the beginning of our relationship."

"Hey, hey save the vows for later, Freckles."

"Peppermint, you haven't seen anything yet." I wink down at her and she grins back at me, free and delighted. I kiss her gently so I don't smear her lipstick, and while I can tell she wants more by the way she grasps my collar and snakes her tongue against mine, I don't want to make love to my wife for the first time in a place that anyone could walk in.

Just then, there's a tap at the door, and our wedding planner, Riley, peeks her head in, smiling at our embrace. "Golden hour is about to hit, ready to get some photos, then dance the night away?"

"Let's do it."

The rest of the evening flies by, and now we're on a plane to Australia where we'll spend the week exploring, making a baby, and trying all the cuisine.

"I'm so tired." Harley groans, rolling her neck as we step into the front door of our hotel room overlooking the Sydney Harbour and Opera House.

"We've been going for a bit between the wedding, travel, and exploring. Want me to get a bath ready?"

"Yes, please." She moans and it goes straight to my cock. I've been ravenous for my wife since we got here, and I'm sure that's not helping her but the way she moans at the prospect of a bath has me ready to forgo that idea altogether.

"Be right back." I step into the en suite, finding epsom salts and bubble bath under the sink before turning on water hot enough for a lobster boil because that's the only way Harley likes to soak.

Once the bathtub is full, I bring my wife into the room, dimming the lights and gently pulling her ponytail loose to release some of the tension in her neck. I help her in before stripping myself and sliding in behind her. The water stings, and I truly don't know how she manages to sit in this for thirty-plus minutes.

"Come here," I grumble, pulling her body into mine and letting my hands knead her shoulders—her body automatically sinking deeper into me and the water.

A quiet contented sigh leaves her lips before she whispers, "You could do this for hours and I wouldn't complain."

"I'm sure you wouldn't." I continue kneading her shoulders until she grabs one of my hands, moving it down her front and onto her chest. Then she grabs the other and moves it to the apex of her legs, guiding my hand exactly where she wants it.

"I want you, Collins." She gasps when I tweak her nipple, her head lolling back and hands seeking my thighs for purchase.

"Thank God," I growl into her neck as I continue to play with her body with my fingers. "I was going to give you a break this evening."

"I don't want that." Her voice coiled tight with need.

"Fuck, me either, Baby." I let two of my fingers push into her entrance and keep my palm pressed against her clit. "Give me one first."

Her body moves against my hand, her grip tightening against my palm until her screams ricochet off the bathroom walls, and her movements have slowed.

"Hands and knees for me, Peppermint."

She obeys immediately, holding herself up against the opposite end of the tub. I don't have the patience to wait any longer, giving her my entire length in one stroke. A pained but pleasured noise leaves her throat.

Our bodies meet thrust for thrust, my hand wrapping around her front to give her the friction I know she needs to give me another one of her beautiful cries. The other is gripping her hip to keep her close to me.

The tingle at the base of my spine becomes more intense as I watch my wife's body begin to tense, thighs shaking as she grips the edge of the tub, and her tight cunt squeezing my cock.

When her pussy tightens around my cock so hard I see

stars, I roar out my release, which tips Harley over the edge, her screams intermingling with my groans.

Catching my breath, I stand and help Harley up, "let's clean up and then bed."

What I thought would be a quick shower turned into Harley on her knees for me and vice versa. Something about the honeymoon phase.

"Best honeymoon ever," she whispers into the dark room when we've finally satiated our need for each other.

Extended Epilogue ‖ Crisis Averted

Harley ‖ Six years later

"**D**ad!" The screech from down the hallway has Collins groaning as he lifts himself from between my legs, where he was enjoying his breakfast because we thought we had more time before our daughter woke up.

"You can't go out there like that." I chuckle, pointing to his crotch, "I got it, hopefully. Depends on what kind of crisis she's experiencing today."

"Thanks, but I'm not done with you." He pecks my cheek as I walk by.

"What's going on, Care?" I ask, entering the kitchen and the scene I'm greeted with has me folded over in laughter. Our daughter Caroline, who was attending the Right Place, Right Time center (not as my patient), joined our family three years ago after we decided that conceiving naturally may not be an option but adoption could be. It didn't matter if I birthed the child; all we knew was we wanted to raise children together. A fellow counselor came to me, expressing that she felt our home was the perfect fit for Caroline, and after months of getting to know her, home visits with the state and court dates, she became ours.

"Mom, it's not funny." She rolls her eyes at me, Precious sits on her shoulder while she tries to flip pancakes on the stove.

"You know, honey, all you have to do is put her on the ground."

"I tried, she keeps jumping up, and I just wanted to make us all breakfast. I'm being nice, you know." She waves a spatula at me like 'duh, mom as if I wouldn't have tried that already.'

I step over, pulling Precious into my arms and kissing my daughter on the crown of her head while I still can— she's grown at least a foot and a half in the time she's been in our care.

"Good morning, thank you for making breakfast. Do you need help?" I ask.

"Nope, I got it. Thanks, Mom."

"Okay, well I'm going to finish getting ready for the day then."

"Finish? Mom, you're still in your mumu."

"I was getting out of bed when a certain teenager started screaming from the kitchen."

"You got me there. Should have the table set in twenty."

"I'll make sure both your Dad and I are out. Love you."

"Love you."

I step into our bedroom to find Collins still sitting on the edge of the bed and set Precious on our floor.

"Crisis averted." I laugh lightly.

"What was it this time?" He asks, pulling me into his lap. "Butterfly in her bedroom? That one boy band broke up... again? She couldn't find her phone? Kendall insisted that Reylo was the ultimate Star Wars coupling again?"

I laugh. I know that last one really irks my husband. His daughter being part of the Star Wars fanverse over Lord of the Rings was almost his undoing. We've convinced her to watch the movies with us but she just doesn't appreciate them the way that we do. At least she's a hockey fan because that really might have sent him into tachycardia.

"Nothing quite so dramatic today. Precious was being a nuisance, and she was trying to make us breakfast." Precious mewls at me as if she knows I'm talking about her before I continue, "Speaking of we need to be dressed and at the table in fifteen."

"So we don't get to finish what we started this morning?" He sighs at me as if I stopped him from working me over earlier.

"We do.... Just later. Parenthood, Baby."

"Fine. Let's shower quickly."

"No shenanigans." I kiss him, quickly heading into our en suite.

"No promises."

"Care! Are you ready? The bus is leaving in ten." I yell toward my daughter's bedroom. We're supposed to be headed up to the cabin that Collins told me he mentally promised me eight years ago for Christmas. Not only did we purchase a cabin, but all of our friends did too, all of which are nearly next to each other, after the annual Christmas trip became a thing.

"Bus? Mom, we're literally getting into Dad's truck to be stuck for like a million hours." She hollers back.

"Not a million. Eight to twelve, depending on traffic. Don't act like you don't love our yearly cabin trip," I say, approaching the entryway of her bedroom where clothes are strewn about as she throws last-minute things into her suitcase and pop music plays out of her phone.

"I do buuuut I hate the car ride."

"Oh, come on, Caroline. It'll be fun," Collins says as he sidles up beside me, throwing an arm over my shoulder.

"Grams and Gramps are going to be here soon, so we need to get packed up." I remind her.

"I'm coming, impatient freakin' parents. Geez." She sasses, thinking we didn't hear her.

"Attitude." Collins and I say simultaneously, checking our daughter and I wouldn't have it any other way.

After Collins' parents arrive and our "million hour drive", we've all pulled up to our cluster of cabins. Everyone is tired from the trip but ready to celebrate Christmas for the eighth year together.

Gathered around the fire, we watch the kids struggle to keep their eyes open so they can hang out past their bedtimes as we sip on spiked apple cider and beers. The kids and young adults sit in a small huddle far enough away to feel the warmth but close enough where they know we can't hear them complaining about being here. One day they'll think of us for this, for giving them these memories and allowing them to experience life in this way.

"I can't believe we've been doing this for ten years already." Kodi sighs into her mug full of spiked apple cider.

"I can't imagine spending our Christmases any other way." Nik agrees, rubbing his beard.

"And one day... They'll hopefully be bringing their kids here in a *very* long time." Darcy tacks on, her voice taking on an emotional tone.

"Alright, let's try not to make ourselves cry tonight." Enid pipes up from where she's perched on Conrad's knee, rubbing a blossoming bump. They got started a little later than everyone else, but Enid was also young when she joined our group, so I don't blame them for waiting.

"Kids, time for bed. Teens turn it in, but you don't have to sleep." Maverick commands of those under the age of twenty, no one looks to their parents for approval because they know we've already decided collectively what time we were all hitting the hay.

Collins and I follow behind Care as she walks to our cabin, clearly invested in some online video or texting conversation. Once we get inside, she scoops Precious up, murmuring goodnight and shutting herself in for the night.

"I can't lie, I miss our view from the A-frame," I mention as I stare out our bedroom window, waiting for Collins to join me for bed.

"This is like, almost an identical view." He grunts, wrapping his arms around me from behind. I relax into his body.

"Sure, but that one holds so many memories for you and I. Before we were us."

"This is true but now we've made different memories, and we'll continue to make memories here."

"Collins?" I say tentatively because I haven't spoken to him about this, but it's been weighing heavily on my heart. I can feel my throat clogging with unshed emotion.

"What's wrong?" He turns me toward him.

"Nothing's wrong. I just... I want to give Caroline a sibling. I want to give another child a home, give them something like this to look forward to. A family to celebrate with."

"Okay, we'll call the adoption agent as soon as we get back." Collins takes my face between his hands.

"You're sure?"

"I am. What I'm not sure about is where you got the impression that I didn't want to continue adding to our family, but I do. Caroline was the most pleasant surprise and there are so many kids like her that need people like you as their mother." He smiles down at me before pulling my face to his, embracing me in his arms. A new memory made right here, in this moment, and many more to come for us.

Also By Katelyn Snyder

Want more from Katelyn?

Want to read Maverick and Kodi's story? Check out ***Shot to the Hart***, book one in the Scoring with Love series on Kindle Unlimited or keep scrolling for the first chapter.

Or are you interested in Tatum and Darcy? **Read *On Three…* *Baby Reed***, book two in the Scoring with Love series on Kindle Unlimited now!

About the Author

Katelyn is a Florida native, born and raised. She lives with her husband, Adam, their daughter and their two dogs, Yogi the goldendood and Smoosh the pocket pittie mix. She's not a fan of being outdoors but enjoys the occasional excursion to the mountains, hoping to one day experience life there. Returning to her love of reading when the COVID pandemic struck, she rediscovered she's a fan of all genres and all things spicy. She gravitates most towards hockey romances while ironically enough she isn't a follower of hockey. Her writing is a labor of love outside of being a stay at home mom. If she's not reading or writing, you can find her playing cozy games on the Nintendo switch, in a Dungeons & Dragons campaign, or binge watching bad reality TV.

Shot to the Hart

Chapter 1-The Sahara

Kodi

Darcy bursts through her front door like the little firecracker she is with... *OH GOD NO*. This bitch has a bottle of tequila in one arm, Harley and Sinclair on the other, and a devious grin on her face. "Get up and get ready hoe. We're drinking and dancing tonight. And before you ask, no, you don't have a choice!" she exclaims, with Harley and Sinclair looking like they will pull me off the couch if I don't willingly get up. My three best friends since high school are on a mission, and once they start, they can't be stopped. If they want to get me off my butt, it'll happen even if they have to drag me out.

"Yeah, no thanks," I say, turning my attention back to my phone where it appears, according to Instagram, that

Andy has been living his best life with Lyla—his coworker. The one he told me not to worry about when we would go out with his colleagues and she'd follow him around acting like I didn't exist. The one who is now spending most of her weekends in the apartment Andy and I lived in together; sleeping in the same bed and on the same sheets that Andy and I spent our nights in. I get why he chose her, she's the opposite of me—bubbly and blonde, skinny, can pull off outfits I wouldn't dare to wear. Probably the exact girl he's always wanted. I juxtapose her in almost every way; my personality isn't big, I have some curves and don't show off all of my assets the way she typically does.

"Ko, it's been two months. I know for a fact you're on one of their pages right now, making yourself miserable when you could be out there, enjoying life with us and gaining your independence back," Darcy states, plopping back down beside me, her blonde hair pulled into a tight pony, her blue eyes crinkling in the corners as she smiles at me. "I'm going to go change and then you are too."

Two months? Wow, I guess I really have been sitting in my miserable, post-breakup mentality.

I've been on autopilot, going to my shifts at *Wake, Bake, Repeat* down the road from Darcy's apartment and then ending up in this exact spot almost every day. Not too long after my breakup with Andy, when I thought *maybe* Andy would take it all back, Bill got an overseas job and offered to move me with them, but at the time everyone was here. Andy was here, and even if we weren't together, I couldn't see myself leaving any of them. After the breakup, I needed a job and fast. Wake, Bake, Repeat was hiring immediately and was walking distance from Darcy's apartment, so I took it.

I need to pick myself up, dust myself off and move forward. I can enjoy a night out with my friends, maybe meet someone new to get under. Andy was my first and only, I fear that I won't be good enough if I give myself to someone else. On the other hand, it could be fun to experience sex with someone different. Worse comes to worst, at least I can get drunk and spend the night dancing with my best friends.

However, now I'm just feeling like a sad, single millennial with no prospects and little to no hope for my future. Sad over this breakup, which is making me feel unmotivated to do anything, including hanging out with my best friends.

If I don't hang out with my best friends then they won't want to be friends with me at all. What's worse than living on your best friend's couch? Moving home with your helicopter Mom because said couch is not an option anymore.

Oh god, being back at home with Mom, who has called almost every day to check-in would drive me nuts. She would never give me a moment of peace and no guy is going to want to date a twenty-four-year-old living at home with her parent. Speaking of Mom, my phone buzzes and I see that she's checking in *again.*

Mom: Hey sweetie, I hope you're doing okay. Let's grab lunch soon.

Me: Just like yesterday, I'm good Mom. We can arrange that. Love you.

Mom: Love you most.

"Ugh, you're right. I need to enjoy life and be more present in this moment." I stand with a determined stride, heading to Darcy's room to make myself presentable. Passing her as she exits in a dress akin to that of a disco ball, she does a little shimmy at me which causes us both to chuckle.

"Where are we going?" I yell in the general direction of where I left my friends.

"Lockout. That new, expensive looking club downtown," Sin says, sidling into the room behind me with two shots in hand. Just like her personality, Sin's hair is fiery red, and she's always looking for trouble. She's sporting a pair of dark wash jeans and a white crop top under a leather jacket that accentuates her chest. Unlike me, she's never been afraid to show off her body and I'm envious of that.

"What's our mission tonight?" Sin asks as I take my shot from her, throwing it back with a wince.

"You guys are the ones dragging me out tonight."

"Well babe, you need to get laid, or at least let someone dance on you. So put on a sexy outfit and let's go find you a man," she says smiling devilishly at me. *Maybe Sin is right, maybe getting under someone else will pull me out of this funk.The thought of being with someone else is scary, but what am I going to do? Be single and sad until I die?*

Even if I don't go home with someone tonight, at least I've taken a step in moving on from my breakup with Andy by enjoying life with my friends. I think back to the night that we broke up and how he said I never wanted to go out or have fun. If he knew that I was headed out tonight would he still think that I was boring, or would he think that I was just trying to prove him wrong? Sure, he was right that I didn't want to go out often—reading and reality TV always sounded like a better option than drinking and dancing—but when I would go out, especially the past few months, he felt detached, barely touching me, not including me in conversations. I should have taken that as a sign that things were not going as well as I let myself believe. I chose to live in my naivety that we were just in a place of contentment and didn't need the same type of excitement we did when we were nineteen.

"Alright, more shots." More shots turned into us killing the bottle of tequila, posting tipsy selfies to our Instagram stories before calling our uber, and giggling the whole drive as we sang off tune to *Please Please Please* by Sabrina Carpenter. Our uber pulls up to the curb of Lockout and I step out wearing a little black dress that I feel confident in, but still covers me in the places I don't typically show off. My patchwork of tattoos are on full display, my jet black hair is curled and falling over my shoulders, and black high tops are on my feet because whoever decided that heels were good for dancing and drinking was actually delusional.

Bodies are packed wall to wall, making me wonder if there's an event going on, or if this is what a Saturday night at the newest club in Tampa looks like. I've been to a few bars and clubs, but I've never seen so many bodies packed into a place like this. The blue, red, and green flashing lights illuminating the dance floor make me realize how tipsy I actually am while dim lights hang over the bar to our left that we are slowly squeezing our way up to.

I'm ready to have a good time with my friends, even though this was not my plan tonight. Honestly, my plan was to cuddle up with my e-reader and a glass of white wine until I eventually passed out.

Harley, with her dark brown curls and bronze skin, sporting a bright pink silky tank and black jeans, leans over into a very handsome, lumberjack-looking man's personal bubble and sweetly asks, "Why is it so busy in here?"

She turns back to me with an eye roll, leaning into my ear and relaying his message, "Why are men the way they are? Tell me why he said, 'Didn't you hear sweetheart? The Tampa Bay Manta Rays took home their first win of the pre-season. Everybody, including some of the players, are here celebrating.' Like dude, you don't have to call me sweetheart and act like I should know what's going on."

"Over there." She gestures towards the VIP section where multiple men are dressed to the nines and flirting with the bottle girls. They all have to be at least 6 feet tall, and some are tattooed, while others have man buns that range from dark to light in color. I can't tell from here, but I'm sure they are more handsome up close. One in particular catches my eye in a navy blue suit, I can really only see his side profile. His hair is longish, golden, and tied half up. His skin is the color of the whiskey he lifts to his mouth, and his suit is tailored to fit his body in all the right places.

I have the sudden need to go and run my hands up his arms—feel how firm they are. I shake it off. I'm tipsy, and surely a hookup with a hockey player is not what I need right now, even if I thought I could get one's attention. I'm just a plain Jane, there's nothing remarkable about my looks or my personality that would snag the attention of someone of that caliber. I'm sure they are only seeking out models or the like. More recently, Andy stopped commenting on how beautiful I was, regardless of much or little effort I put in. The only people who ever hyped me up were my best friends, and they are required to do that by friendship law.

I decide to ignore all thoughts of the men standing in the roped-off section and focus on spending time with my friends. I drag them out onto the dance floor and dodge the hands of grabby men. After what feels like hours of dancing, I grab Sin and drag her to the bar with me. While we wait to squeeze to the bar top, I pull up my phone and two notifications stick out. Andy liked my story, and I have a text from him.

Andy: Glad to see you're spending time with your friends, you look good. Been thinking about you.

What the fuck. I haven't heard from him once until right now and now he's suddenly thinking about me.

I don't have time to decide if I want to respond because Sin is grabbing my wrist and pulling me up to the bar. We order a round of shots, taking them back to Harley and Darcy. We throw them back, wincing as the alcohol slides down our throats, then return to dancing. The night continues on and we drink enough to know we are all waking up hungover tomorrow.

Just as we decide this is probably going to be our last song of the night, a pair of hands find my waist, and a warm body presses into my back. The feeling of someone else's hands on me after five years of only Andy's has me almost shrugging the touch off, but Sin's words from earlier come back to me. I remind myself that I need to get laid or at least have fun with someone. Instead of pushing him off, I turn away from my wide-eyed friends who are clearly shocked by the fact that I am allowing this man to touch me. I give myself over to the feeling of dancing with him and let myself enjoy the feel of his hands on me. He's handsome, probably an accountant or business man, taller than my five-four by what could be three, four, maybe five inches, and his eyes meet mine with a devious glint in them.

"Hey there, beautiful, I'm Conrad," he finally says, leaning into my ear.

"KJ," I reply in a sultry tone before turning my back to him and allowing myself to lean into him as we continue to dance with my friends surrounding us. Giving him Andy's nickname for me allows me some anonymity, he doesn't need to know Kodi because he will probably never see me again after tonight.

We dance for another five songs before I feel his hot breath against my neck and hear him over the music as he asks, "Wanna get out of here?"

I nod and signal my friends in the direction of the exit. We reconvene on the sidewalk outside of the club.

"Where are you taking her?" The first question thrown in Conrad's direction, from Harley, as everyone orders their Uber rides home. Everyone ordering their rides makes me question one last time if I want to do this or hop into the car my friends are taking and maybe see what Andy is doing.

Nope, no, not doing that, I don't need to go down that path again. Conrad it is.

"I'm staying at The Edition about fifteen minutes away," he hesitates, "room three seventeen."

"If she doesn't come home tonight, and I don't get a text

from her when you arrive at your hotel, I will find you, and I will make sure your dick is irreparable. Got it, Conrad?" Darcy smiles up at Conrad who has an arm around my waist, holding me close.

"And I'll make it look like an accident," Sin slurs from her seated position on the sidewalk, head hanging in her hands.

"She's not joking, she knows how." Darcy's smile is now more evil than sweet. My best friend likes to think she is a pitbull, but she's more of a dachshund. She can bite your ankles, but won't do much more damage than that.

"Let us see your ID," Harley pipes up beside Darcy, arms crossed over her chest. Conrad raises an eyebrow at her, but she doesn't back down.

"Alright, you win," he chortles, pulling his ID out and handing it over. Harley snaps a quick pic and hands it back to him.

"Oh, Uber's here, babe. Ready?" He gestures in the direction of the silver sedan waiting on the side of the road. I give a quick hug to my friends and slide into the car beside Conrad.

Twiddling with my hair, leg gently bouncing, I ask Conrad, "So, what do you do for work?

He laughs as if I said something funny. "I play hockey, KJ, for the North Carolina Firestorm. We lost to your team, the Manta Rays, and some of the guys wanted to blow off steam, maybe find a bunny to take back to the hotel." He eyes me up and down. *Is he insinuating that I'm a puck bunny?* "We just didn't realize Lockout was the celebration spot for the home players."

"No fucking way." My response is almost immediate. "I

wouldn't know that you're a player. I don't keep up with sports."

Just as our Uber pulls up to the hotel, Conrad scoffs, almost a little offended that I didn't know who he was. Shrugging it off, I slide out of the Uber with Conrad placing a hand on my back to guide me, quickly sending a text to the girls that we made it to the hotel.

The elevator ride is quiet, Conrad subtly moving his hand lower until he's got a handful of ass. When the door dings open, he guides me to his room, scanning his card and gesturing for me to enter.

Walking further into the room, Conrad approaches me placing his hands on my shoulder and turns me to face him. Moving one hand up to the back of my neck, he hauls me to him, our lips meeting in a fevered crash as he unzips my dress with the other. He guides us backward, laying me down and spreading my legs with his.

"Fuck. You are a sight." Leaning back on his haunches to completely undress us both then rolling a condom on that he very clearly had in his pants pocket.

I'm starting to regret my decision to come back with him. *Let's hope he can make me come, that's the least he can do. Although it wouldn't be the first and probably won't be the last time a man put his pleasure before mine.*

He lines himself up with me, pushing in, and then he's moving in wild, erratic movements. He doesn't kiss me, tries to find my clit but fails miserably, and five minutes later, we are laying next to each other with Conrad's arm wrapped around me, a look of pure bliss on his face while I am drier than the Sahara.

Turning to Conrad I say,"I had fun tonight, maybe I will

catch you next time you guys play in town." With a frown that he quickly shakes off, he gets out of the bed and says," Yeah of course. I did too. Let me walk you to the elevator and grab your number."

And with an awkward side hug, I head back to Darcy's apartment, so not ready to share the details of the night but knowing full well I will have to.

Acknowledgments

I published my third book all while navigating being a first time mom! I am so incredibly proud of myself so go me!

Now onto the people that helped me get here in no particular order.

To my critique partner, Mindy Pettengill. Mindy, as always your feral reactions and valuable feedback helped to turn Have Yourself a Merry Little Collins into the story that I envisioned. You also helped me with promotion, hyping up my posts, bringing my art to life and being an all around support system since our goldfish brains get along so well. Thank you putting up with my nonsense everyday and being a best friend- the Devil couldn't find me so he put you across the country.

To my alphas, Kris, Jensen, and Ryan. Thank you all for your excitement as you read Have Yourself a Merry Little Collins! You each brought incredible feedback and encouraged me when I felt this story wasn't at it's best.

To my betas, Allison, Bailey, Chachi, Cierra, and Jessie. Thank you for taking the time to beta read for me, your feedback always helps to shape the stories of my characters.

To Harley, my PA. Thank you, thank you, THANK YOU! For being my brain when pregnancy brain got the best of me, for incredible graphics and brainstorming that's helped my reach! I'm excited to grow with you by my side.

To my parents, I'm sorry that you can't read this book either even though I know you'll have a signed copy on your shelf I can't thank you enough for your love and support my whole life, like when I decided to play softball or joined the winterguard team with no athletic ability you encouraged me to practice and grow everyday. That encouragement is what led me to finish my second book and publish it knowing you would be proud of me.

To Adam, my husband, the sunshine to my grumpy and my knight in shining tin foil. When I looked at you and said I'm writing another book, you as always encouraged me to keep writing. When I was stressing again over deadlines, costs of services and about actually publishing for people to see my book with their eyeballs, you continued to tell me how proud of me you were and that no matter what people thought, I did it and I should be proud of that too. I love you so many.

To my real life Darcy, aka Em. Half of our lives and you still give me unconditional support and I couldn't do it without you.

To my Chaos Crew, thank you all for sharing, liking, and reposting. For letting me bounce ideas off of you, for hyping me and both my book babies up before they was even in your hands,

for deciding where spicy scenes should take place and helping expand the book playlist. You all are amazing!

Lastly to my readers, this is my third book and if you've read it well I can't thank you enough. I didn't think people would be excited about my first book, let alone my second and now the third but there were more people than I could imagine who wanted to meet my characters and you being one of them just makes my day! I hope you stick around for what's next in the Scoring with Love series.